EVANGELISM IN THE SUNDAY SCHOOL

LEADERSHIP TRAINING SERIES

1. **Standard Training Course.**—A series of studies in the religious needs and capacities of persons of all ages and in ways of dealing with those needs and capacities by means of an effective program of religious education.

2. **Bible Course.**—The units of this course are Bible units of a content nature.

3. **Missions and Social Service Course.**—This course deals with the interpretation and practical application of the Christian religion.

LEADERSHIP TRAINING SERIES
STANDARD TRAINING COURSE

EVANGELISM IN THE SUNDAY SCHOOL

BY

E. B. CHAPPELL, D.D.

---

*APPROVED BY THE GENERAL SUNDAY SCHOOL BOARD OF
THE METHODIST EPISCOPAL CHURCH, SOUTH*

WILDSIDE PRESS

PRINTED IN THE UNITED STATES OF AMERICA

DEDICATION

TO MY DEAR FRIENDS AND LONG-TIME
FELLOW WORKERS

DR. CHARLES D. BULLA

AND

DR. JOHN W. SHACKFORD

TO WHOSE COUNSEL AND COÖPERATION
I AM LARGELY INDEBTED FOR WHATEVER SUCCESS
I HAVE ATTAINED IN MY EFFORTS TO
MAKE THE SUNDAY SCHOOLS OF
THE METHODIST EPISCOPAL CHURCH, SOUTH,
REALLY EFFECTIVE EVANGELISTIC
AGENCIES, THIS VOLUME IS

AFFECTIONATELY DEDICATED

CONTENTS

7

CHAPTER I

WHAT IS EVANGELISM?

THE first requisite for the successful prosecution of any task is that the worker shall have a clear understanding of what he is seeking to accomplish. One is not likely to land at a given destination who simply starts out traveling without any definite idea as to the locality of the place to which he wishes to go or the way by which he is to reach it. And the Sunday school teacher is not likely to prove an effective evangelist who has hazy or erroneous notions as to what evangelism is. Let us, therefore, begin our studies by endeavoring to come to an understanding as to what we mean by evangelism.

I. ORIGIN AND MEANING OF THE WORD "EVANGELISM"

No Greek equivalent of the word "evangelism" is found in the New Testament. Three kindred words are found, however, which it may be worth while for us to study. These kindred words are:

1. The noun *evangelion*, the original meaning of which was simply "good news." In the New Testament it meant at first the good news that in the person of Jesus of Nazareth the long-expected Messiah had at last appeared and was about to establish his kingdom on the earth. Later it came to comprehend all that the Christ meant for the individual and for the world. The English word by which it is translated in the King

9

James Version is "gospel," derived from two Anglo-Saxon words, one meaning "good" and the other "a story."

2. The verb *evangelizein*, generally used as a deponent middle either with or without an object. Used in the former way it means to proclaim something as good news, as when Jesus says, "I must preach the kingdom of God to other cities also" (Luke 4: 43), and when it is said of the early disciples at Jerusalem, "They ceased not to teach and to preach Jesus Christ" (Acts 5: 42). Literally the former means "I must proclaim as good news the kingdom of God to other cities also," and the latter "they ceased not to proclaim as good news Jesus as the Christ."

Used without an object, the word simply means to proclaim the good news as interpreted in the preceding paragraph.

3. The noun *evangelistes*, which in our common English versions is not translated at all, but is simply brought over in Anglicized form. It means literally "a bringer of good tidings." The word is used three times in the New Testament: In Acts 21: 8, where Philip is spoken of as "the evangelist"; in Ephesians 4: 11, where evangelists are included among the recognized officials of the apostolic Church and are distinguished from apostles, prophets, and pastor-teachers; and in Second Timothy 4: 5, where St. Paul exhorts Timothy to "do the work of an evangelist."

Our information in regard to the mission of the New Testament evangelist is derived mainly from what we know about the work of Philip and of Timothy. The

10

little that is told us about the work of Philip (see Acts 8: 5–40) reminds us rather strikingly of the work of the modern evangelist. Indeed, it is often assumed that he conducted a series of religious services in Samaria and perhaps in other places very closely resembling the "revival" meetings conducted by modern evangelists. The assumption, however, is only partially correct. Perhaps the main features of resemblance between the work of Philip and that of the man whom we speak of as an evangelist are that Philip had no fixed field of labor and that his primary aim was to win unbelievers to faith in Christ rather than to instruct and edify believers. It is quite clear, however, that the missions of both Philip and Timothy were primarily to those who had not heard the gospel before. In other words, they were missionaries rather than evangelists as we now understand the term.

It is evident from this study that the derivation of the word "evangelism" furnishes only a slight clue as to its significance in current usage. Literally it means the act of proclaiming the good news, and it is sometimes used in this sense, as, for instance, when we speak of evangelizing the world in a single generation. Such an expression cannot, of course, mean that we expect really to make the world Christian in a single generation. Indeed, we have never yet succeeded in making any single nation on the face of the earth more than partially Christian. All we can possibly intend, therefore, when we use the words "evangelism" and "evangelize" in this way, is to call the Church seriously to undertake the task of immediately proclaiming the

11

good news throughout all the world and of establishing Christianity as a vital working force in every nation. When, however, we speak of evangelism in the Sunday school, it is clear that we have in mind something much deeper and more far-reaching than merely telling people about Christ. Evangelism, in other words, as the term is here employed, implies very much more than the term itself, considered in the light of its derivation, would suggest.

II. The Mission of the Church

Perhaps a better way of approach is to begin with a brief study of the mission of the Church and how it is to be accomplished.

1. The mission of the Church is to build up the kingdom of God until it shall attain final and complete triumph. "After this manner therefore pray ye: Thy kingdom come. Thy will be done, as in heaven, so on earth." In these words our Lord reveals to us the ultimate purpose of his Church, and in praying this prayer we commit ourselves to his program and pledge ourselves to become coworkers with him in carrying it out.

2. The kingdom of God is a social order, a great brotherhood over which God is recognized as Father King and in which social relations are regulated by the law of love. But no program of social reconstruction can succeed that does not begin with the individual. A brotherhood must be composed of brotherly men. A society in which the will of God is done must be made up of people whose inner lives are in harmony with God

12

and who seek increasingly to understand what the will of God is. No social covenants or legal arrangements, either national or international, can secure peace, justice, and coöperation so long as men are selfish and unbrotherly.

3. Hence, while the ultimate aim of the Church is the establishment of a world-wide Christian social order, its immediate and fundamental task is the making of Christlike men and women.

In our insistence upon the social aspect of the mission of Jesus we must not overlook the fact that it was also a mission to individuals. "I came," he said, "that they may have life and may have it abundantly" (John 10: 10). A fine commentary on what the abundant life of which our Lord speaks is may be found in one of St. Paul's great prayers:

> For this cause I bow my knees unto the Father, from whom every family in heaven and on earth is named, that he would grant you, according to the riches of his glory, that ye may be strengthened with power through his Spirit in the inward man; that Christ may dwell in your hearts through faith; to the end that ye, being rooted and grounded in love, may be strong to apprehend with all the saints what is the breadth and length and heighth and and depth, and to know the love of Christ which passeth knowledge, that ye may be filled unto all the fullness of God. (Eph. 3: 14–19.)

Another passage from the writings of the same apostle furnishes a striking picture of the way in which this inner spiritual life may be expected to express itself in social relations. Indeed, a fitting title for the paragraph would be "The Christian in His Social Relations."

13

Let love be without hypocrisy. Abhor that which is evil; cleave to that which is good. In love of the brethren be tenderly affectioned one to another; in honor preferring one another; in diligence not slothful; fervent in spirit; serving the Lord; rejoicing in hope; patient in tribulation; continuing steadfastly in prayer; communicating to the necessities of the saints; given to hospitality. Bless them that persecute you; bless, and curse not. Rejoice with them that rejoice; weep with them that weep. Be of the same mind one toward another. Set not your mind on high things, but condescend to things that are lowly. Be not wise in your own conceits. Render to no man evil for evil. Take thought for things honorable in the sight of all men. If it be possible, as much as in you lieth, be at peace with all men. Avenge not yourselves, beloved, but give place unto the wrath of God; for it is written, Vengeance belongeth to me; I will recompense, saith the Lord. But if thine enemy hunger, feed him; if he thirst, give him to drink; for in so doing thou shalt heap coals of fire upon his head. Be not overcome of evil, but overcome evil with good. (Rom. 12: 9–21.)

A society composed of men and women possessing the qualities of life which these passages describe would speedily find ways of solving all the more serious of its perplexing social problems. To raise up such men and women, therefore, is the primary business of the Church.

III. Material Out of Which the Kingdom Is To Be Built

The material out of which citizens of the kingdom are to be made is that which is found in our common human nature with its mingled assortment of capacities and limitations.

1. That man is endowed with **moral and religious** capacity there can be no question.

14

(1) So he is represented throughout the Bible. We are told that in the beginning he was created in the image of God, and this evidently refers not to his body, but to his real self, the self that thinks and loves and recognizes the supremacy of moral law. That this likeness, though marred, has not been destroyed by the fact of sin is witnessed by the oft-repeated moral and religious appeals which God makes to men in the Bible. For these appeals are without meaning except upon the assumption that there is something in man answering to the divine call to worship and to obedience to the moral law. Take, by way of illustration, the oft-quoted invitation found in Revelation 22: 17: "The Spirit and the Bride say, Come. And let him that heareth say, Come. And let him that is athirst come. And whosoever will, let him take the water of life freely." Such words would be mere mockery if addressed to a being destitute of moral and spiritual capacity or of ability to respond to the gracious invitation.

(2) And this teaching of the Bible is confirmed by the whole course of human history. For the pages which record the story of man are not altogether black. On the contrary, gleams of light as if from heaven often irradiate them; for they tell of a ceaseless search for truth, for God, for spiritual emancipation, and of unnumbered deeds of heroism and self-sacrifice for love's sake and for conscience' sake. The Psalmist gives utterance to a yearning that is as old as the human heart when he says:

> As the hart panteth after the water brooks,
> So panteth my soul after thee, O God.

15

And Tennyson puts into words what millions of souls of all lands and ages have felt when he makes Sir Galahad sing:

> I yearn to breathe the airs of heaven
> That often meet me here.
> I muse on joy that will not cease,
> Pure spaces clothed in living beams,
> Pure lilies of eternal peace,
> Whose odors haunt my dreams.

Such longings after God and such visions of spiritual beauty are perhaps far from being universal, but that they have been felt by multitudes of elect men and women in all lands and all ages there can be no question.

2. This, however, is only one side of the story. There is another side that is dark and sinister of aspect.

(1) The Bible opens with the majestic account of man's creation in the likeness of God. But after this comes the story of his disobedience and fall, and then follows an endless record of selfishness and greed and lust and cruelty, of moral struggles ending in defeat and longings after moral triumph ending in disappointment. Perhaps the most striking picture of the inner aspect of this age-long conflict is found in St. Paul's account of his own experience in Romans 7: 15-25a. For the sake of vividness I use Weymouth's translation:

For what I do, I do not recognize as my own action. What I desire to do is not what I do, but what I am averse to is what I do. But if I do that which I do not desire to do, I admit the excellence of the law, and now it is no longer I that do these

16

things, but the sin which has its home within me does them. For I know that in me, that is, in my lower self, nothing good has its home; for while the will to do right is present with me, the power to carry it out is not. For what I do is not the good thing that I desire to do; but the evil thing that I desire not to do is what I constantly do. But if I do that which I desire not to do, it can no longer be said that it is I who do it, but the sin which has its home within me does it. I find therefore the law of my nature to be that when I desire to do what is right evil is lying in ambush for me. For in my inmost self all my sympathy is with the law of God; but I discover within me a different law at war with the law of my understanding, and leading me captive to the law which is everywhere at work in my body—the law of sin. (Unhappy man that I am! who will rescue me from this death-burdened body? Thanks be to God through Jesus Christ our Lord!).

(2) This pathetic description of the futile inner struggle of the great apostle is typical of universal human experience. The literature of the world is full of it— moral aspiration on the one side and on the other the humiliating sense of sin and failure. Tennyson makes one of his characters cry out in passionate longing:

> And O for a man to arise in me,
> That the man I am may cease to be!

And Whittier makes his sad confession in stanzas that find an echo in every earnest heart:

> More than your schoolmen teach, within
>   Myself, alas! I know,
> Too deep ye cannot paint the sin,
>   Too small the merit show.
> I bow my forehead in the dust,
>   I veil mine eyes with shame,
> And urge, in trembling self-distrust,
>   A prayer without a claim.

The Biblical explanation of all this is that man is the victim of an evil inheritance, and that, as a consequence, the tendency in every one of us to go astray is so strong that he finds himself constantly unable to do the good which he would and constantly practicing the evil which he would not.

IV. THE SECRET OF SPIRITUAL TRIUMPH

The Bible is at one with universal human experience in its teaching in regard to man's evil inheritance and moral impotence. It is unique, however, in the fact that it offers a remedy and points out a way of escape. It will be observed that St. Paul's account of his own ineffectual struggle quoted above ends with an exclamation of thanksgiving for deliverance. He had at length found the secret of victory over his lower self which he had hitherto sought in vain.

1. When we come to inquire what was the secret of this marvelous emancipation, we find that the apostle attributes it to the power of the indwelling Christ. "It is no longer I that live," he declares, "but Christ liveth in me" (Gal. 2: 20). To the Roman he writes, "If Christ is in you, the body is dead because of sin; but the Spirit is life because of righteousness" (Rom. 8: 10), and in his message to the Colossian Christians he uses the significant expression, "Christ in you, the hope of glory" (Col. 1: 27). The same thought appears in Hebrew 3: 14 ("For we are become partakers of Christ") and in Second Peter 1: 4 ("He hath granted unto us his precious and exceeding great promises, that through these ye may become partakers of the

18

divine nature"). And Jesus himself had already revealed the possibility of such an experience. In John 17: 23 he speaks of being *in* his disciples, and in John 6: 54 he says, "He that eateth my flesh and drinketh my blood hath eternal life." "Flesh" and "blood," as the words are here used, are the symbols of life. To eat his flesh and drink his blood, therefore, is to become a partaker of his life. Hence he immediately adds, "He that eateth my flesh and drinketh my blood abideth in me and I in him." (John 6: 56.) The entire passage is to be interpreted, not literally, but mystically and spiritually.

For an individual to become a partaker of the life of Christ so that he can say "Christ liveth in me" is to be "born anew" in accordance with the word of Jesus to Nicodemus in John 3: 3. The fact that Jesus speaks of the Holy Spirit as the agent in this process of spiritual quickening need not trouble us. The Godhead is not divided either in essence or action. Where the Father is there the Son is, and where the Son is there the Holy Spirit is, and where the Holy Spirit is there the Father and the Son are. When Jesus was about to go away he said to his bewildered disciples: "I will not leave you desolate; I will come unto you." (John 14: 18.) But a little farther on in the same conversation he speaks of sending the Holy Spirit to bear witness of him. That is, in the person of the Holy Spirit he would come unto them and "abide with them always." Indeed, so absolute is the divine unity that we find St. Paul declaring that "The Lord is the Spirit" (2 Cor. 3: 17), and in Romans 8: 8–10 he speaks almost in the same breath of the indwelling Spirit and the indwelling Christ as if they amounted to the same thing: "And they that are in the flesh cannot please God. But ye are not in the flesh but in the Spirit, if so be that the Spirit of God dwelleth in you. And if Christ is in you, the body is dead because of sin."

2. The sum of it all is that through the indwelling life of God our higher natures may be so quickened and recruited that we become new creatures in Christ Jesus, walking not after the flesh but after the Spirit. All deeply spiritual men have testified to the reality of this mystical experience and have found purification and emancipation through the incoming and indwelling of the divine Spirit. "All the glory and beauty of Christ," says Thomas à Kempis, "are manifested within, and there he delights to dwell." John Wesley defines religion as "the life of God in the soul of man." The best possession of the human soul," declares Bishop Warren A. Candler, "is the indwelling Christ."

SUGGESTIONS FOR STUDY

1. What light do the derivation and literal meaning of the word "evangelism" throw on its meaning in present usage?

2. What further light do we get from a study of the mission of the Church?

3. Show that the gospel message is both individual and social and explain why it is so.

4. Wherein lies the secret of spiritual triumph?

CHAPTER II

WHAT IS EVANGELISM (CONTINUED)?

THE discussion in the preceding chapter ended with the statement that the power by which we are cleansed and quickened and enabled to live the triumphant life is the power of the indwelling Christ. This at once suggests the inquiry as to how we are to come into the possession of this transforming power.

I. SACRAMENTARIANISM, LEGALISM, AND INTELLECTUALISM

1. There are many who hold that it is communicated by a process that is akin to magic. This is the fundamental implication of all theories that make regeneration dependent upon some rite performed in some particular way by a properly accredited ecclesiastical agent. The priest administers the sacramental ordinance in the manner prescribed and pronounces the sacred formula in the name of the Holy Trinity, and forthwith the miracle is accomplished, the soul of the subject is cleansed from sin and he passes out of death into life. Such an assumption is contrary to reason as well as to the cardinal teachings of the New Testament and has no rightful place in Christianity.

2. There are others who think of spiritual life as mechanically imparted as a result of conformity with certain legalistic requirements or of the intellectual acceptance of certain credal statements. There are

wide divergencies of opinion among those maintaining these views as to what observances and beliefs are required, but they agree in interpreting religion in terms either of legalism or intellectualism; and the positions which they hold, whether they realize it or not, necessarily involve the assumption that spiritual life may be arbitrarily and mechanically communicated.

These are precisely the errors into which the Pharisees of our Lord's day had fallen. They were literalists and legalists, putting the main emphasis in their religion upon the correctness of their opinions and their strict conformity to the letter of the ceremonial law. But Jesus pronounced them mere actors, and compared them to "whited sepulchers, which outwardly appear beautiful, but inwardly are full of dead men's bones and of all uncleanness." (Matt. 23: 27.) And there is a negative as well as a positive lesson in the parable of the Good Samaritan, which clearly implies that there is no essential connection between credal affirmations and legalistic observances and the purification of the inner life.

The first serious controversy in the Christian Church, as we learn from a study of the Acts and the Epistle to the Galatians, was over this very matter. (See Acts 15: 1–29 and Galatians 2.) An influential faction of Jewish Christians maintained that, in order to be saved, one must observe the entire Mosaic ritual, and insisted, therefore, that it was necessary that Gentile converts should be circumcised. This contention St. Paul opposed with all the might of his inspired genius, and it was through his influence that the Church was saved

22

from becoming a Jewish sect, bound in the fetters of a mere mechanical legalism.

We escape all the errors mentioned above when we come to think of salvation in terms of positive moral and spiritual attainment by free personal agents and of religion as a means through which free agents are enabled to achieve Christlike character and fit themselves for Christlike service. There is a deep sense in which salvation is the free gift of God. He *gave* his only-begotten Son for our redemption, and the benefits of his sacrificial death and his triumphant life are offered to all without money and without price. But these benefits cannot be arbitrarily bestowed. Spiritual life is not a semimaterial something which exists apart from personality; it is rather a quality of personality and can be communicated and received only by vital processes that are in accord with the laws which condition the life of free personal agents. God is a person, and we are persons created in his likeness, and all of his dealings with us must be in harmony with the laws governing the relations of free personal beings.

II. RELIGION AS A PERSONAL RELATION

These considerations suggest the secret of all spiritual attainment. The soul is cleansed and quickened by the birth from above, the gift of divine life through the Holy Spirit, and we come into the possession of this gift through an immediate personal relation with God.

1. That such a relation is possible is one of the most precious assurances given to us in the Bible. "Enoch walked with God." Abraham "was called the friend

23

of God." "Jehovah spake unto Moses face to face, as a man speaketh unto his friend." The prophets communed with God and reported to the world the messages they had received in fellowship with him. In his last conversation with his disciples before his crucifixion Jesus said unto them, "No longer do I call you servants, . . . but I have called you friends." (John 15: 15.) In the apostolic benediction which we so often hear St. Paul teaches us to pray for "the communion of the Holy Spirit"—that is, that the conscious presence of the Holy Spirit may be shared by all. And St. John, in his First Epistle, says: "Our fellowship is with the Father and with his Son Jesus Christ."

Nor is this a privilege which was granted only to a few rare souls selected out of the Hebrew race, but a privilege offered freely to every member of the human family who will fulfill the conditions of friendship. In a strikingly beautiful passage found in Revelation 3: 20 Jesus is represented as saying: "Behold, I stand at the door and knock: if any man hear my voice and open the door, I will come in to him, and will sup with him, and he with me." Supping together in the ancient oriental home was a sign and pledge of friendship. What our Lord is here saying in substance, therefore, is: "I am always seeking to establish relations of personal fellowship and friendship with every man and woman and child, always seeking access to every human heart." Those who seek to become his friends cannot fail, since he is ceaselessly seeking to become the Friend of every one.

2. It is through such a personal relation as is implied

24

in real friendship that God is enabled to impart his life unto us. Jesus said to his disciples, "I am the vine, ye are the branches." (John 15: 5.) The connection between the branch and the vine is not mechanical, but vital, and through this vital connection the life of the vine flows into the branch. So is the life of Christ communicated unto us when we come into a vital relation with him. Hence he tells his disciples that if they abide in him he will abide in them, and that, as a consequence of this union, they will bear much fruit.

3. The only thing that can vitally unite person with person is faith, a twofold bond of trust and love. St. Paul speaks of it as "faith working through love." There are persons whom we pass frequently without being in the least influenced by them, because our relation to them is purely external. We never come in contact with their souls, their real selves. So we are always in the presence of God. "In him we live and move and have our being." And yet God cannot in the richest and fullest sense communicate his life unto us until through faith we come into a relation of vital personal fellowship with him. Faith, therefore, is not an arbitrarily established condition of salvation, but a condition that grows out of the fundamental nature of personality. It is God's only way of vital access to free moral agents and therefore the only medium through which his saving grace may become efficacious for them. (Eph. 2: 8.)

4. It should be observed, however, that the faith that saves is not the intellectual acceptance of a creed, but loving trust in and self-committal to a Person.

25

It is the duty of the Christian to seek by prayerful study, by fellowship with the risen Lord, and by fidelity in doing the will of the Father in heaven to rid himself of erroneous opinions and to widen and deepen his understanding of all that is involved in the personality and teaching and work of Christ. But one who is not a Christian cannot afford to postpone beginning the Christian life until one has worked out what one regards as an adequate system of theological beliefs. The correct order is precisely the reverse of this— namely, for the seeker to begin by submitting himself to God as he is revealed in Jesus and then by the process suggested above to develop a rich and vital Christian creed. Of course one must know something about Christ before any intelligent committal to him can take place, but, as a rule, the beginning of the new life is the spontaneous emotional response of the soul to the appeal of Christ's personality, rather than the acceptance of a system of doctrine as the result of an elaborate process of investigation and reasoning.

When Saul surrendered to Christ on the Damascus road it is probable that all he knew about the earthly life of Christ was what he had picked up from current rumor and what he had learned through contact with Stephen and from hearing Stephen's dying message. He had before him, therefore, only a mere outline of the Master's work and personality, but that was enough to destroy his Pharisaic complacency and fill his soul with profound unrest and unutterable longings. And "when it pleased God to reveal his Son in him" through the light that shone upon him out of the heavens and

26

the voice of yearning compassion that spoke to him, forthwith his heart surrendered, and he became at once and forever the bondslave of Christ. "The heart," says Pascal, "has reasons of its own." In the realm of the spiritual it goes before the natural reason and shows it the way. So it was in St. Paul's case. It was after his conversion that he went into retirement in Arabia to think out the meaning of this new and marvelous experience.

5. It should be remembered, however, in considering the intellectual compulsion under which St. Paul found himself to give a rational account of his new allegiance and his new experience, that he was a man of remarkable intellectual ability. The average man is under no such compulsion. His heart surrenders to the appeal of the personality of Christ, he finds in Christ the satisfaction of his spiritual longings, and, like Thomas, he cries out in adoration, "My Lord and my God!" But when it comes to metaphysical discussions in regard to the person of Christ and to theological discussions in regard to the work of Christ, his interest ceases. Such matters are beyond the range of his comprehension, and all his efforts to think them through simply end in confusion.

Doctor Chalmers, one of the great Scotch preachers of the nineteenth century, tells the following story: A plain woman came before the session of a certain Church to be examined for admission to Church membership. The dignified elders asked her a number of questions which she was unable to answer, and it soon became apparent that the decision would probably be against her. She was profoundly disappointed, and, looking at them out of tear-dimmed eyes, she sobbed out: "I can't explain him, but I'd die for him."

There are millions of Christians like that. They know Christ as a personal Saviour and follow him with adoring love; but when it comes to explaining him, they are as much at a loss as they would be if called upon to explain the chemical process by which the light and warmth of the sun waken the dormant life of the vegetable world in springtime and cause the seed to spring up and grow and blossom in beauty and bring forth fruit.

And it is often true even in the case of men of broad culture and unusual intellectual ability that the beginning of their allegiance to Christ is a matter of the surrender of the heart to his personality rather than a matter of reasoned conviction.

In a volume of lectures by Doctor R. W. Dale entitled "The Living Christ and the Four Gospels" there is a chapter on "The Divine Appeal of Christ to the Spirit of Man." In this chapter the author tells about a conversation he had had a few years previous to the time of its writing with a Japanese Christian who was noted for the breadth and thoroughness of his scholarship as well as for the dignity and nobility of his character. In the course of their talk together Doctor Dale sought to find out from his Japanese friend how it was that he became a Christian. "I reminded him," he says, "that he and his countrymen were wholly separated from the traditions of Christendom and from that unbroken line of historic continuity by which we ourselves are united to those who first received the

28

Christian gospel. I also reminded him that, although the thought and civilization of Western Christendom had recently been exerting an immense and revolutionary power in Japan, the Christian faith had not come to his people unchallenged; that in the foremost nations of Europe the historical trustworthiness of the story of Christ had been assailed by men of great eminence; and that, side by side with Christianity, there had come to the Japanese a varied and powerful literature which impeaches its claim and calls upon Christian nations to surrender their faith as an illusion. I then asked him by what path he had reached his faith in the Lord Jesus Christ as Son of God and Saviour of men."

In reply his friend told how he had been brought up a Confucian, how Confucianism had failed to satisfy the deepest needs of his soul, how at length a Japanese convert to Christianity had given him a Chinese Bible and asked him to read it and how profoundly impressed he had been with such inspired messages as the thirteenth chapter of Paul's First Epistle to the Corinthians. "And then," he added, "I read the Gospel of John, and the words of Christ filled me with wonder. They were not to be resisted. I could not refuse him my faith."

Upon this testimony Doctor Dale comments as follows: "The vision of glory which came to him while reading John's account of our Lord's life and teaching was a vision from another and diviner world; he fell at the feet of Christ, exclaiming, 'My Lord and my God!' . . . He *saw* the divine majesty and the divine grace of Christ: what could he do but worship him?"

29

III. The Fundamental Aim of Evangelism

The conclusions to which the preceding discussion leads us may be summarized as follows:

1. Religion is fundamentally a matter of personal relation. It is friendship with God as he is revealed in Jesus Christ. Jesus said to the Pharisees: "Ye search the scriptures, because ye think that in them ye have eternal life; and these are they which bear witness of me; and ye will not come unto *me*, that ye may have life." (John 5: 39, 40.) Notice particularly the closing sentence in this statement, *"Ye will not come unto me, that ye may have life,"* the clear meaning of which is that Bible study is of no avail if it does not bring us into an immediate personal relation with Christ. Compare with this the following significant utterance in our Lord's great intercessory prayer: "This is life eternal, that they should know thee the only true God, and him whom thou didst send, even Jesus Christ." (John 17: 3.) Compare also this striking utterance of St. Paul in Philippians 3: 8, 9: "I count all things to be loss for the excellency of the knowledge of Christ Jesus my Lord: for whom I suffered the loss of all things, and do count them but refuse, that I may win Christ and be found in him."

2. Since evangelism, as the word is used in these studies, is the process of making Christians, and since men are delivered from the dominion of the lower self and enabled to live as sons of God and citizens of his kingdom through union with Christ, the fundamental aim in all of our evangelistic efforts should be

to bring people of all ages, classes, and conditions into a vital personal relation with Christ. This conclusion is in complete harmony with the Great Commission, according to which the primary business of the Church is to make disciples. "Disciple" literally means "learner." Long before the time of Christ, however, it had come to be used in a semitechnical sense. A disciple was a person who had attached himself as pupil and intimate friend and companion to some master teacher in whose wisdom and goodness he thoroughly believed, his aim being not only to learn from the master's lips, but also to come in ever-increasing measure under the ennobling influence of his personality. A Christian disciple, therefore, is one who has become thus related to Jesus Christ, the one absolutely supreme and authoritative Teacher and the one all-sufficient Friend "whom to know aright is life eternal." This means, of course, that discipleship as describing the Christian's relation to Jesus stands for something much deeper and more vital than anything that can possibly be involved in the relation of a pupil to a mere human teacher. For it means absolute trust and absolute surrender to one whom we revere as Lord and Saviour.

3. It should be observed, however, that the Great Commission does not stop short with the command to go and make disciples, but adds two other significant clauses, "baptizing them in the name of the Father, and of the Son, and of the Holy Spirit; teaching them to observe all things whatsoever I commanded you." (Matt. 28: 19, 20.) Real friendship is never static. Friendship must either grow or decay. Every great

31

friendship is the result of a process of growth. Friendship with God is no exception to this general rule. Hence St. Peter exhorts Christians to "grow in the grace and knowledge of our Lord and Saviour Jesus Christ." (2 Pet. 3: 18.) And St. Paul, even so late in his life as the time of his first imprisonment in Rome, still felt that his knowledge of Christ was as nothing compared with what yet remained to be learned. He writes as one who is just beginning to get a clear vision of what friendship with the Master really involves. Read Philippians 3: 7-14, and notice how he emphasizes by repeating it again and again his longing to know Christ—to know him more intimately, more thoroughly, more vitally.

In the Great Commission, therefore, our Lord lays upon his followers the duty, not only of making disciples, but also of providing for them the conditions of a growing intimacy with him and a growing understanding of him and of increasing efficiency in service. To this end they are to see that every beginner in the Christian life, by receiving the ordinance of baptism, openly declares his discipleship and becomes definitely affiliated with the Church which is the body of Christ. And then they are to proceed step by step to instruct him in the teachings of Christ and to train him in the practical applications of these teachings in everyday conduct.

The evangelistic work of the Church, in other words, is not to cease when the individual whose salvation she is seeking has been led to enter upon the Christian life, but she is to continue to work with him and for him that she may lead him step by step toward the realization of the ideal of St. Paul, "a complete man of God, furnished completely unto every good work."

4. In thinking of the experience described in this and the preceding chapter, let us put the primary emphasis upon the positive aspects of it. Evil tendencies are not overcome by a mere process of repression, but by the quickening and development of the nobler capacities of the soul through friendship with God and through continuous normal exercise in the service of God. Children go wrong, in other words, not only because they are the victims of an evil inheritance, but also because they have not been brought into that relation of loving fellowship with God which is the rightful heritage of every one of them and without which no moral being anywhere can come to fullness of spiritual life. The worst result of sin is that, by separating the sinner from God, it renders moral recovery impossible, and one of the supreme advantages that we find in dealing with childhood lies in the fact that no such positive alienation has taken place. There are both good and bad tendencies within him, but both are mere potentialities, the awakening and development of which depend upon the appeal of influences from without. It is the business of the home and the Church, therefore, to avail themselves of the opportunity thus offered to bring the child into living fellowship with God that his moral and spiritual capacities may be awakened and quickened by the Holy Spirit before the evil tendencies within him have been awakened and strengthened through contact with the world and through actual transgression.

3   33

SUGGESTIONS FOR STUDY

1. Explain the sacramentarian and legalistic views of regeneration and show why neither is tenable.

2. What does the Bible teach in regard to the possibility of friendship with God?

3. What is the result of such an immediate personal relation with God?

4. Why is faith a necessary condition of salvation?

5. What is the faith that saves?

6. Explain what is meant by religion as a personal relation.

7. Consider how the views here presented harmonize with the teaching of the Great Commission.

8. When does the evangelistic process come to an end?

34

CHAPTER III

EVANGELISTIC AGENCIES

I. First Steps in Evangelism

THE conclusion of our previous study was that the aim of evangelism is to bring individuals into a living fellowship through faith with Jesus Christ, and to provide the conditions of a growing knowledge of and friendship with Christ and increasing efficiency in the service of Christ.

1. The initial step in this process must be the preparation of the individual for receiving the revelation of Christ. For, as it was necessary to prepare the way for the Lord's entrance upon his Messianic work, so it is necessary to prepare the way for his entrance into a human heart. The response which we desire to the appeal of Christ is at once a religious and an ethical response, and of course such response is possible only as the religious and moral nature is awakened. To bring about such awakening, therefore, must be the first aim in our evangelistic efforts. This, of course, means one thing in the case of the little child and quite another in the case of the adult who has fallen into sinful habits, but this is a matter for future consideration.

2. Along with the preparation of heart and mind must go such a revelation of Christ as will beget within those whom we seek to save a living faith in Christ and will lead them to surrender their lives to him. I have already called attention to the fact that the beginning

of the Christian life is not a matter of accepting a set of theological opinions, but rather a matter of the spontaneous surrender of the soul to the appeal of Christ's personality and spirit and ideal. "In many cases," says Doctor James Bissett Pratt, "getting converted is falling in love with Jesus." If "getting converted" is understood in the sense in which it is employed in common religious terminology, we should not be far wrong in saying that getting converted is *always* falling in love with Jesus. Recall once more the circumstances attending the conversion of Saul of Tarsus, noting the fact that it was not the result of his theology, but that his theology was rather the product of his Christian experience. It was by the revelation of the risen Christ that the heart of the bitter persecutor was subdued and made captive.

And the only unique features connected with the case of Saul are its external attendants. The history of the Church, and especially the history of modern missions, furnishes innumerable instances of striking conversions brought about solely through the immediate appeal of the personality of Jesus. Recall the story told by Doctor Dale in regard to the conversion of an educated Japanese.

The central aim in our evangelistic efforts, therefore, should be to win the hearts of those whom we seek to save through the revelation of Christ.

3. It should be observed that the two processes described above—namely, the awakening of the religious and moral nature and the revelation of Jesus Christ—are not to be thought of as things entirely

independent of each other, but as largely coalescing with one another. That is, we do not first seek to awaken the religious and moral nature of the individual and then to make Christ known to him, but we seek progressively to make Christ known as an essential part of the process of bringing about the individual's moral and religious awakening. In other words, we seek at the same time and through the same means to make him both religious and Christian.

II. Agencies Employed in Evangelism

Let us now proceed to a consideration of the chief agencies that are to be employed in the process described above.

1. The first of these both as to time and effectiveness is *personality*.

(1) The beginning of the religious awakening of the little child, as a rule, is the result, not of formal religious instruction, but of the influence of the spirit and attitude and acts of his mother. For, just as the child responds to the love or joy or sorrow written in the face of his mother or expressed in her bearing or in the tones of her voice, so he responds to the spirit of faith and reverence that shines out through her eyes and manifests itself in all sorts of subtle ways in her speech and conduct.

(2) Nor does this influence of personality lose its potency as the child advances in years. Not for the young only, but for people of all ages and all degrees of culture Christlike character remains the most convincing and irresistible witness for Christ. It speaks

directly to the soul in language that all but the desperately depraved can understand, and there is no arguing against it.

A missionary was preaching to a group of natives in a remote Chinese village. As he was picturing the life of the Christ who came from heaven to tell men about the Father and save them from sin, his hearers began to cry out in the congregation that they knew him, that he had lived among them and taught them and been their personal friend and helper. The missionary tried to explain to them why they must be mistaken, but they still insisted that they had seen the great Friend and knew him. And, by way of convincing him that they were right, they took him at the close of the service to their cemetery and showed him a rude board upon which was written the name of a medical missionary who had lived in the village some years before. During his residence the town was visited by a terrible plague, and many fell victims to its deadly influence. All the wealthy families who could do so ran away, leaving the less fortunate to get along as best they could. But the medical missionary remained with them and comforted and served them until he too was smitten by the dreadful malady and carried away. And so, when they heard again the story of the loving, self-forgetting, serving Christ, recalling the life of this martyr friend, they said, "We have seen him." And they were right, for through the words and deeds and personality of his heroic and devoted servant Jesus had really revealed himself unto them.

A group of scientists were talking with each other

about the agencies that had been most potent in leading them to accept the Christian faith. Finally one of them, who had been listening in silence to his companions, spoke in substance as follows: "Gentlemen, none of the things you have mentioned had anything to do with making me a Christian. I was convinced and led to accept Christ through the influence of my Christian wife. In her character I found a kind of evidence which I could neither answer nor withstand."

(3) That is the kind of witness which is always most needed. There is no other revelation of Christ that is so irresistibly convincing and so vitally effective as the personality of one who lives the Christ life. Teachers of religion may as well understand that they cannot create the kind of atmosphere of love and reverence that is needed for the awakening of the religious nature of the child unless they themselves are truly religious and that all their teaching about Christ will be of but small avail in making Christ real to their pupils unless they reflect in some measure the image of Christ.

I read recently a bitter attack on Christianity by a man who tells us that his father was a Sunday school superintendent and his mother an active worker in the Woman's Missionary Society, and that in his childhood he attended church and Sunday school and was often associated with preachers. But unfortunately he found in none of these any of the winsomeness and spiritual beauty of Christ. Instead, his father seems to have impressed him as a profane hypocrite, the missionary meetings as centers of neighborhood gossip, and the preachers as lacking in that kind of virility, sense of fair play, and spirit of comradeship which every normal boy admires. The story suggests its own lesson.

One of the encouraging things connected with the work of the Church to-day is that teachers of religion are at last beginning to awaken to the fact that they cannot successfully discharge their responsibilities relating to the evangelization and religious development of the young without intelligent preparation. It is very important, however, that they do not forget that there is one essential part of this˙ preparation which they can get only through intimate fellowship with God and faithful obedience to his will for us as revealed in Jesus.

2. To the revelation through personality must be added interpretation through definite instruction.

(1) The child must be told *about* the heavenly Father whom his parents and his teachers love and trust and obey and to whom he is indebted for all the precious gifts of life, and the ideal of Jesus must be progressively revealed to him through stories that are within the range of his comprehension and that are adapted to his life needs. Through teaching, in other words, the child must learn to see in the goodness and love which he finds in his parents and teachers a reflection of the goodness and love of God, and his vague impressions must be transformed into definite convictions and a vital personal faith.

(2) And what is true of the child is equally true of the adult who has not become a positive Christian. It is futile to call such an one to surrender to Christ until he knows something about who Christ is and to

what manner of life he calls us. A beginning in such knowledge may be made through observing the life of a Christlike man or woman, but only a beginning. The picture thus drawn in vague and imperfect outline must be filled out through study of the life and teachings and works of the Master himself.

(3) Christianity has from the beginning been a teaching religion. Jesus himself was the supreme Teacher. The title most commonly applied to him in the New Testament is "teacher." "To this end," he says, "was I born and for this cause came I into the world, that I should bear witness unto the truth." (John 18: 37.) And when he commissioned and sent forth his disciples it was with the command that they should go and *teach*. Teaching is one of the great agencies, not only for spreading the evangel, but also for interpreting its deeper meanings and showing how it fits into the needs of individual life and how it affects our everyday duties and our social relations.

(4) For the purpose of this study preaching may be regarded as a type of teaching. It differs from teaching, as usually understood, in that it is less systematic and more impassioned. Real preaching has in it somewhat of the prophetic element. That is, it is an authoritative proclamation of truth that has been immediately revealed to one's own soul or verified in one's own experience. It becomes at once apparent, therefore, that all real preaching must also be teaching and that the most effective teaching must have in it some of the fervor growing out of the immediate vision and personal experience that characterize the best type of preaching.

There is no difference as to aim between teaching and preaching. Both seek to influence the lives of individuals by lifting up Christ before them and bringing home to them in a vital and convincing way the meaning of his mission and message.

(5) It goes without saying that if teaching is to have a large and important place in the evangelistic work of the Church, it is her bounden duty to make the most thorough possible preparation for discharging her teaching ministry.

She must expend whatever is required for equipment in the way of libraries, lesson material, and buildings, to the end that her teachers may be provided with favorable conditions and proper tools for their work.

She must raise up an adequate force of prepared teachers. And by prepared teachers I mean those who know Christ, who know their Bibles, who know those to whom they are to minister, who know how to mediate unto them the truth as it is in Christ Jesus, and who are filled with an ardent evangelistic passion.

And, as it is the imperative duty of the Church to equip herself for her great teaching task, so it is the d'ity of every Christian who is called to this sacred ministry to "give diligence to show himself approved unto God, a workman that needeth not to be ashamed, rightly dividing the word of truth." And by "rightly dividing the word of truth" I mean dividing it in such way that each may receive in due season the food that is adapted to his needs and that it may be served in such a way as effectively to meet these needs.

3. Another agency in evangelism is atmosphere.

By atmosphere I mean the general spirit which pervades a given group of people, a family, a Church, a community. It is not easy to define, but everybody recognizes its existence and is more or less cognizant of its influence.

You occasionally go into a home in which you discern at once the signs of order, cheerfulness, and reverence, and of mutual respect and consideration between all the members. Your whole nature responds at once to its stimulating and invigorating influence, and you instinctively say to yourself, "How fine and wholesome for boys and girls!" For you know that it is just the kind of place in which seeds of truth planted in the mind will spring up and grow and bear fruit.

There are other homes into which you go in which the pervading spirit is quite the opposite of this. Instead of order, you find confusion; instead of reverence, shallow cynicism; and instead of mutual respect and consideration, either bickering or indifference. And, whatever may be the relation of the parents in such a home to the Church, or their attitude toward religion, you expect to find their children undisciplined, disrespectful toward their elders, and devoid of that reverence for God which is the beginning of wisdom.

I recently read a story about some rare varieties of date trees that were imported from Africa a few years ago by the Government of the United States. The scientists who were in charge of these trees planted them first in a certain locality in California. While, however, they lived and grew after a fashion, they did not bear fruit. Then another locality was tried, but

43

with the same result. Finally they were taken to the Coachella Valley, and the atmospheric conditions there proved to be just what they needed. They not only grew luxuriantly, but bore abundant fruit.

Proper atmosphere is just as essential to the development of spiritual life as it is to the development of plant life, and it is the business of Christian parents and Christian teachers to see that such atmosphere pervades the home and the Sunday school, since without it all their efforts to make lasting, spiritual impressions upon those whom they seek to teach the way of the Lord are likely to prove ineffective.

In our efforts to create a proper atmosphere physical conditions must be taken into consideration. Children respond readily to their physical surroundings. It is much easier to teach effectively in a neat, clean, quiet room, properly lighted and ventilated, than in a dismal and disorderly basement or in an auditorium filled with noise and confusion. We can hardly expect to inspire children with respect for what we are trying to do if we have not sufficient interest to cause us to have the same care for the building that is dedicated to the worship of God and to religious education that we have for our own homes. On the other hand, successful work may be done even in a small one-room church, if the classes are separated by screens and if the building and grounds are kept neat and in good repair.

But much more important than the physical surroundings is the spirit that animates the membership of the Church and especially the leadership of the Sunday school. That spirit must be, first of all, one of love and cheerfulness and reverence. And where such a spirit exists it will show itself in regularity and promptness of attendance on the part of the officers and teachers and in their whole bearing toward each other and toward the school and the classes. Officers and teachers who habitually come to their work late or poorly prepared, or who are lacking in courtesy, calmness, and self-control, cannot create the kind of atmosphere in the Sunday school that tends to awaken the interest and to command the respect of the pupils. It would be well if these matters were more frequently discussed and made subjects of earnest prayer in the Workers' Council, to the end that the officers and teachers themselves might develop a unity of aim and purpose and discover the most effective ways of coöperation in creating the most favorable conditions for the awakening and development of the spiritual life of the pupils.

4. One of the essential factors in a proper atmosphere for the Sunday school, as has already been suggested, is the spirit of reverence. It is not easy to maintain such a spirit in a group made up largely of children and youth. For children and youth are not naturally reverent. The spirit of reverence must be developed in them by wise and persistent training. Hence a very important factor in the program of educational evangelism is the worship service. This should be studied both by the superintendent and the teachers with the greatest care. Every worship service, whether for the separate department or the school as a whole, should be thoroughly planned in advance with a definite purpose of

45

meeting the religious needs of the pupils and securing their vital and intelligent participation.

5. Protestantism is right in maintaining that salvation is a matter of grace and not of works, and yet properly directed and motivated service may be a very effective agency in the kind of evangelism which we have in mind. What we are seeking in all our evangelistic efforts is to produce religious impressions and to develop religious attitudes, and one of the means for accomplishing this is that of opening up for those whom we wish to lead into the religious life ways of giving proper expression to the feelings awakened within them through our teaching. Truth becomes real and vital only as it is expressed in conduct. There have been many instances in which mature men and women, who had remained indifferent in the face of all sorts of appeals, have been converted by being induced to take part in some kind of religious activity in the Sunday school. And it is especially necessary in the case of children that impressions shall be deepened and fixed by expression. The teacher must not only seek to reveal Christ and the Christ ideal to his pupils, but he must seek also to discover for them adequate ways for expressing the love and loyalty awakened within them. For only thus may their faith in him and their allegiance to him be vitalized and established.

6. The Bible everywhere teaches that there is power in prayer, that God hears and answers prayer. No teacher will be successful in leading her pupils to Christ who does not constantly and earnestly pray for them—

not as a group but as individuals, each having his own peculiarities and his own special needs.

III. ADAPTATION OF AGENCIES

In the use of the agencies described above the teacher must observe fundamental educational principles. The teaching through which the religious and moral nature of the child is awakened and through which the child is brought into a vital personal relation with Christ must be real teaching. And this means that all teaching agencies and methods must be adapted to the capacities and needs of those who are taught. The teaching material must be within the range of their understanding and must be presented in a way that will appeal to their normal interests, and in the case of children programs of worship and activity must be such as will make a vital appeal to the child mind. It goes without saying, therefore, that the effective teaching evangelist must know his pupils and must study to find the easy passage to the heart of each one of them.

SUGGESTIONS FOR STUDY

1. What are the first steps in the evangelistic process?
2. Mention the chief agencies in evangelism and give a brief explanation of each of them.
3. Which of these agencies do you regard as most effective? Why?
4. Explain the differences between preaching and teaching and discuss the advantages and limitations of each.
5. How may a proper atmosphere be created in a Sunday school?
6. What is meant by expression as an agency in evangelism?
7. Discuss the place of prayer in evangelism.

CHAPTER IV

EVANGELISTIC METHODS

ALL of the evangelistic agencies described in the preceding chapter are employed in all kinds of evangelistic effort, but the way in which they are employed and the degree of emphasis that is placed upon one or another of them are determined by the types of persons whom we are seeking to save.

The Church from the very beginning of her ministry has made use of two methods of evangelism. These methods are commonly designated as the educational method and the revival. It should be observed, however, before these methods are described, that they are not mutually exclusive, but that at many points they coincide. For instance some of the important features of the revival are employed by the Sunday school in its annual special evangelistic campaigns, and every successful revival must be partly the result of an educational process lying back of it. And yet there is a sufficiently wide difference between the two methods to justify their separate consideration.

This chapter will be devoted to a study of educational evangelism.

I. EDUCATIONAL EVANGELISM DEFINED

The aim of all true evangelism is the same—namely, to awaken the moral and religious nature, bring the individual into vital union with Christ, and promote his spiritual development by helping him to attain an ever-deepening knowledge of Christ. Educational evangelism seeks to accomplish this by an educational process—that is, it seeks through the continuous and adapted use of all legitimate evangelistic agencies to promote the development on the religious side of the intellect, the emotions, and the will in their relation to Jesus Christ, and his claim upon the individual life. It recognizes the continuous growth of religious understanding and the ripening of religious appreciations and convictions and sees all of this as immediately related to what is termed "decision for Christ," which, in its final form, may be the act of a moment or the gradual attainment of a fixed Christian attitude.

Please observe that, according to this definition, educational evangelism does not represent an attempt to produce Christian character without divine quickening and coöperation, but that its aim is to secure such quickening and coöperation as a condition of all real spiritual attainment. In other words, its aim is not to enable people to get along without Christ, but to bring them to Christ and to help them to attain an ever-deepening knowledge of Christ, "whom to know aright is life eternal."

II. A Fundamental Assumption

Any program of educational evangelism must of necessity be based upon the assumption that man is endowed with both religious and moral capacities and that these are subject to the same laws that condition all his other native endowments. That is, if they are

4   49

supplied with proper atmosphere, proper nurture, and proper opportunities for expression, they will awaken and develop, thus making the individual in reality a religious and moral being. It is true that complete moral development can come about only by sharing the life of Christ through faith, but in the absence of moral capacity there could be no response to the appeal of the personality and teachings of Christ; and the awakening of the moral as well as the religious nature is, therefore, a necessary part of preparing the individual to accept Christ. The point to get clearly in mind is, however, that the above assumptions imply that every normal child may become the subject of moral and religious education and that it is possible by an educational process to prepare the way for the incoming of Christ into his heart as well as to promote the development of his spiritual life after he has definitely accepted Christ.

Attention has already been called to the fact that the affirmation that man, even in his fallen state, possesses religious and moral capacity is supported by the teachings of the Bible as well as by the study of human life and history. Inasmuch, however, as this view has for fifteen centuries been stoutly challenged by a large and influential section of the Church and inasmuch as the matter is of fundamental practical importance, it may be well for us to pause for a somewhat more careful examination of the opposite contention and the reasons for rejecting it.

1. The system of doctrine which is known in the modern Church as Calvinism was first fully elaborated and defended by Augustine, Bishop of Hippo, in North

Africa, who lived from 354 to 430 A.D. The fundamental article in Augustine's creed was that of the absolute and unconditioned sovereignty of God. This led naturally to a complete denial of the free agency of man. Man is a mere puppet in the hands of an omnipotent autocrat, who orders everything according to his sovereign will. Whatever happens comes about according to his arbitrary purpose and decree.

Contradictory as it may appear, however, Augustine taught also that Adam, although utterly impotent and helpless, by his fall not only brought the whole human race under legal condemnation, but also brought about the complete destruction of man's moral nature, leaving him not simply destitute of moral capacity, but actually and innately wicked. That is, the child is not so constituted that he may become wicked. He is born so. For original sin, according to Augustine's interpretation, is much more than an inherited moral taint or tendency to evil which must be counteracted by divine grace. It is real guilt of the deepest and blackest kind. The doctrine of infant damnation follows as a logical conclusion. "The infant who is lost," says Augustine, "is punished because he belongs to the mass of perdition and, as a child of Adam, is justly condemned."

At the time of the Reformation John Calvin, a brilliant French theologian, adopted and elaborated the views of Augustine and brought them over into Protestantism. Calvin teaches concerning children that "they bring condemnation from their mother's womb" and that "they are odious and abominable to God."

51

2. It would seem that a system of doctrine so repugnant to reason, so contrary to the observed facts of life, and so completely out of harmony with the revelation of God in Christ Jesus would meet with instant and universal condemnation in our modern world. As a matter of fact, however, although Calvinism in its grosser forms is no longer generally accepted, it still has a profound influence upon the religious thought of the Christian world. There are millions of people who do not regard themselves as Calvinists, but whose views in regard to such important matters as child nature and child nurture and the meaning, conditions, and consequences of the new birth are nevertheless largely determined by Calvinistic presuppositions. This is one of the reasons why Protestantism has always given religious education a subordinate place in her program and has never even seriously attempted to develop a consistent and thoroughgoing system of Christian nurture and training. For it is evident that, if the Calvinistic view of human nature is accepted, the idea of religious education becomes an absurdity except in the case of those who have already been regenerated.

And it is because of the paralyzing influence of this widespread heresy upon the most important part of the great practical task of the Church that I deem it worth while to give it an amount of attention that I should not otherwise regard as necessary. It is time that Methodists, at any rate, were ridding themselves of the lingering influence of this monstrous survival of medieval theology and fully and intelligently accepting all the implications of their Arminian creed.

(1) This creed, in the first place, is in harmony with the fundamental teachings of the Bible. The God who is revealed in Jesus Christ is not an arbitrary tyrant, but a loving Father. And throughout the Bible, in both the Old and New Testaments, man is recognized as a free agent, endowed with religious and moral capacity, and therefore capable of responding to religious and moral appeals. Without such capacity the whole divine revelation would be meaningless. For what is the Bible, after all, but the record of God's providence in the religious and moral education of the Chosen People, and of his continuous and patient appeal to men as free moral agents to seek deliverance from sin by coming into living fellowship with him and surrendering their hearts and their wills to him? Herein, as has already been suggested, lies a very important part of the meaning of the incarnation. It is the culmination of God's effort so to reveal himself to his bewildered and doubting and erring children as to win their trust, their love, and their passionate devotion. "God was in Christ, reconciling the world unto himself"; "God so loved the world that he gave his only-begotten Son, that whosoever believeth on him should not perish, but have everlasting life."

It is true that, according to the teaching of St. Paul, this does not exhaust the meaning of the atonement. For even Arminian theologians admit that the great apostle teaches a doctrine of the federal headship of Adam. They emphatically deny, however, that his teaching bears any resemblance to that of Augustine and Calvin. Paul maintains that, since Adam was the

53

father of the race, his transgression resulted (a) in bringing the whole race under legal condemnation and (b) in so tainting human nature as to make it impossible for any one without divine help to attain inner harmony and complete moral triumph. But he also teaches that through Jesus Christ provision is made for meeting both of these difficulties. That is, he maintains that through the work of Christ legal acquittal is secured for the entire race and provision made for counteracting the moral effects of the fall and for the offering of full and free pardon to every actual transgressor. (See Romans 5: 15–21; 1 Cor. 15:22.) The inferences from St. Paul's teaching may be summarized as follows:

(a) No one is born under legal condemnation.

(b) The little child belongs to the kingdom of God and, if kept in the right kind of atmosphere and supplied with proper nurture and training, may, as his intellectual and spiritual nature unfolds, be brought into such a personal relation with Christ that he will become progressively a "partaker through faith of the divine nature, having escaped the corruption that is in the world through lust." And in that case, although he may have his seasons of doubt and may sometimes yield to temptation, he may never know himself as other than a child of God.

(c) The prodigal who has left the Father's house and wasted his spiritual substance in riotous living, through repentance and faith, may obtain pardon and cleansing and be restored to his forfeited birthright.

(2) All this is in accord with the historic position of

54

Methodism as interpreted in the writings of its early leaders and as authoritatively set forth in its doctrinal standards.

(a) It is not claimed that early Methodist theologians saw and accepted all the implications of the Arminian creed which they adopted. The Church in which they grew up had been dominated for more than a thousand years by the theology of Augustine, and it would have been practically impossible for them all at once entirely to rid themselves of its influence. But they rejected its fundamental contentions and at least pointed out to their successors the direction in which the theological thought of the future was bound to move. They taught the universality of the divine fatherhood and love, the universality of the atonement, and the universality of the offer of the gracious privilege of coming through faith into a saving friendship with Jesus Christ. They taught also that man is a free agent, that he is endowed with capacities which make it possible for him to respond to the appeal of moral and spiritual ideals, and that his destiny, therefore, is determined, not by divine decree, but by his own voluntary choice.

Commenting on Romans 5: 18, John Wesley says: "We conceive that, as through the obedience and death of Christ the bodies of all men become immortal after the resurrection, so their souls receive a *capacity of spiritual life and an actual spark or seed thereof.*"

John Fletcher takes pains to show that when St. Paul speaks of certain men as having been "dead in trespasses and in sins" (Eph. 2: 1) he does not mean that their moral capacities had been utterly destroyed,

55

but that the word "dead" is used "to denote a particular degree of helplessness and inactivity *very far short of the total helplessness of a corpse.*" And it should be remembered that the apostle in the passage referred to is not speaking of the state of children as they come from the hand of God, but of adults who have been rescued by the power of Christ from lives of sin.

Adam Clarke, after showing that "many" in botn clauses of Romans 5: 15 ("For if by the trespass of the one the *many* died, much more did the grace of God, and the gift by the grace of the one man, Jesus Christ, abound unto *the many*") includes every human being, adds that the passage as a whole means that "saving grace is tendered to every soul, and a measure of divine light is actually communicated to every heart."

And Doctor James Whedon, a distinguished Methodist theologian of the last century, whose Commentaries were widely used by Methodist preachers fifty years ago, comments as follows on Romans 5: 18: "From Adam's offense resulted condemnation *upon all men;* from Christ's righteousness justification (in the sense of legal acquittal) *upon all men.* The condemnation would have produced exclusion of the race from existence by the infliction of immediate death upon Adam. But the glorification by the atonement secured the continuity of the race by which *every person comes into the world in a justified state.*"

Quotations of similar import might be multiplied almost without number. These are sufficient, however, to show that the views which are here advanced are all necessarily implied in the fundamental assumptions of Arminian theology and in their essential features have from the beginning been advocated by the great interpreters of Methodism.

(b) The clearest authoritative interpretation of the position of the Methodist Episcopal Church, South, in regard to the nature of the child is found in our ritual for the baptism of infants. The ritual opens with the following exhortation to the congregation:

"Dearly beloved, forasmuch as all men, though fallen in Adam, *are born into this world in Christ the Redeemer*, heirs of life eternal and subjects of the saving grace of the Holy Spirit; and that our Saviour Christ saith, 'Suffer the little children to come unto me, and forbid them not, for of such is the kingdom of God'; I beseech you to call upon God the Father through our Lord Jesus Christ, that of his bounteous goodness he will so grant unto this child, now to be baptized, the continual replenishing of his grace, *that he may ever remain in the fellowship of God's holy Church*, by faith that is in Jesus Christ."

The prayer which comes immediately after this address begins as follows: "Almighty, ever-living God, we beseech thee for thine infinite mercies that thou wilt look upon this child, sanctify him ever with the Holy Ghost; that, *abiding safe in the ark of Christ's holy Church*, and being steadfast in faith," etc. And finally, in the admonition to the parents of the child, they are reminded that it is their bounden duty to attend diligently to his religious education and are required to promise that "when he hath reached the age of discretion, he being willing thereto and showing

57

evidence of a living faith in Christ," they will bring him before the congregation, that he may ratify and make his own the act of "dedication" implied in his baptism.

Doubtless isolated passages may be quoted from the Bible which seem to favor the Calvinistic position; but it is so repugnant to reason and so thoroughly contrary to the teachings of Jesus that an ever-increasing number of modern Christians find themselves under an intellectual compulsion to seek for some other interpretation of these passages than that which Calvinism places upon them. John Wesley, who was one of the most tolerant and catholic men that ever lived, declared that the God of Calvinism was worse than the devil, and when the advocates of the doctrine affirmed that they could prove it from the Bible, his reply was: "Will you prove by the Scripture that God is worse than the devil? It cannot be. Whatever the Scripture proves, it cannot prove this; whatever its true meaning be, this cannot be its true meaning. Do you ask, 'What is its true meaning then?' If I say I know not, you have gained nothing; for there are many Scriptures the true sense whereof neither you nor I shall know till death is swallowed up in victory. But this I know, better it were to say that it had no sense at all than to say that it had such a sense as this." The plain meaning of this statement is that Wesley found the teachings of Augustine and Calvin so contrary to reason and so thoroughly out of harmony with God's revelation in Christ that no array of proof texts and arguments could convince him of their truth.

58

(3) What John Wesley found impossible in his day is certainly not less so to those who are one hundred and fifty years farther away from the influence of the outworn and discredited social, political, and theological beliefs of the medieval world, and have had one hundred and fifty additional years in which to study in the free atmosphere of modern Christian democracy the teachings of Jesus and the moral and religious history of mankind. For while this study reveals to us inveterate evil tendencies in man, it reveals to us also the existence of capacities and aspirations which answer to the challenge of "the high calling of God in Christ Jesus." The literature of all lands and ages is filled with the records of man's religious longings and of his struggles for moral achievement. "If you will take the pains to travel through the world," says Plutarch, "you will find towns and cities without walls, without letters, without kings, without wealth, without money, without theaters and places of exercise, but there never was seen by any man any city without temples or gods." And this broad declaration has been abundantly confirmed by modern investigation. Doctor Livingston tells us that he found no tribe in darkest Africa that did not have some kind of religion. Doctor George A. Coe, in "Education in Religion and Morals," after speaking of reports circulated a generation or two since about certain tribes that were supposed to be entirely without religion, adds: "But the tribe destitute of religion is found to be purely imaginary. Man has a religious nature. The definite establishment of this

59

proposition is perhaps the greatest service that the history and psychology of religion have performed."

And this conclusion is in harmony with the observations of all those who have had dealings with child life. Sympathetic and intelligent teachers practically without exception bear testimony to the fact that there is no appeal to which the little child responds more readily than to the religious and moral appeal.

III. WHEN EDUCATIONAL EVANGELISM IS MOST EFFECTIVE

1. The meaning of the conclusions stated in the preceding paragraphs is that there is no bar, either legal or moral, to the effective religious education of the child.

The legal condemnation under which, according to the teaching of St. Paul, the whole race was brought by the sin of Adam is completely removed through the sacrifice of Christ. The only condemnation, therefore, under which any one rests is that which he brings upon himself by voluntary transgression, and, since the child has been guilty of no transgression, he is free from condemnation.

The child inherits certain evil tendencies which can be overcome only through divine grace, but he possesses also moral and religious capacities which through divine grace may be quickened and developed until he comes to fullness of spiritual life in Christ Jesus. And these capacities are subject to precisely the same general laws and conditions as to their awakening and growth as are all other native capacities of the soul.

The conclusion to which we are necessarily led, therefore, is that the supreme opportunity for effective educational evangelism is in childhood and youth. For the facts here stated, when carefully examined, will be seen to involve two things, both of which are deeply significant:

(1) The child in the beginning responds as naturally and readily to the right kind of moral and religious appeal as the embryonic life wrapped up in the seed responds to the genial warmth and refreshing showers of spring. The heart of the child who is physically and mentally normal is always good ground. It has neither been hardened by neglect nor corrupted by evil habits nor warped from the truth by error and prejudice.

(2) This condition of plasticity and spontaneous responsiveness, however, continues for a relatively short time. The universal law relating to the soul's native capacities is that if their cultivation is entirely neglected they soon begin to dry up and tend toward a condition of more or less complete atrophy. And this tendency, as it relates to religious and moral capacities, is almost sure, in the case of the neglected child, to be hastened by the formation of sinful habits and blinding prejudices.

As a result of these facts the early years of the child's life are by all odds the most important; and, if his religious nurture and training are neglected during these years, it is difficult by any subsequent effort to make up for the loss thus incurred. This explains the fact that at least seventy-five per cent of Church members join before they reach the age of twenty-one and that practically all of those who become Christians after they are twenty-one received some measure of religious training in early life, either in the home or in the Sunday school, or in both.

Some years ago I chanced to be alone for half an hour with a lad who was perhaps between twelve and fourteen years of age. Knowing something of the social group to which he belonged, it occurred to me that I might undertake, without being impolite or unduly obtrusive, to find out what his attitude was toward religion. The result of my investigation was the discovery that he had never been a member of any Sunday school, had attended only one religious service in his entire life, had never read a chapter in the Bible nor uttered a prayer, and that no sort of religious influence of any kind whatever had been brought to bear upon him in his home. When I asked him, in conclusion, what he thought would become of him when he died, he replied that he supposed he would go down into the ground. In other words, so far as I could ascertain, he was entirely without religious convictions and practically destitute of religious feeling. I know nothing about the subsequent history of this lad, but I am quite sure that if the neglect of which he had been the unfortunate victim was continued for five or six years longer he reached a point where he was practically inaccessible to any kind of religious appeal.

And social workers tell us that they find many cases that are even more serious than this. That is, they find children in their early teens who have already learned to sneer at religion and morality and who hold the Church in contempt.

It is quite certain that but few if any of those who are converted in our revivals are drawn from these neglected classes, since the inevitable consequences of such neglect is to destroy the responsiveness to religious and moral appeal which is so strikingly characteristic of early childhood.

In a recent survey of religious education in the State of Indiana, made under the direction of Dean Walter S. Athearn, it was found that of the 1,693 Sunday school teachers who answered the questionnaire one-fourth joined the Church under twelve and six-tenths years of age and that only one-fourth joined after the age of seventeen and six-tenths. It is probable that if a wider survey were made it would be found that this is about the average for the entire country. The inference from these facts is inevitable. If the Church is to build up a triumphant kingdom of God on the earth by Christianizing the individual members of society, it must attend diligently and intelligently to the evangelization of childhood and youth. And the only proper method for such evangelism is the educational method.

2. It must not be assumed, however, that educational evangelism is entirely inapplicable in the case of adults.

(1) As has already been suggested, it may be reasonably assumed that most adult conversions, however and whenever they may be brought about, are in some measure the results of a previous process of religious education. The conversion of Saul of Tarsus was sudden and was the immediate result of the miraculous manifestation of the risen Christ; but back of it were a long course of religious instruction and training in

63

home and synagogue, impressions in regard to Jesus of Nazareth which must have come to him through current report, and impressions which he certainly received as he listened to the final message of the martyr Stephen and witnessed his triumphant death. And it was through this educational process and these awakening influences that his heart was made ready for the call which came to him as he journeyed toward Damascus.

(2) In St. Paul's case, although there was a previous process of preparation, the final surrender was brought about through an overwhelming, dramatic appeal. It is possible, however, to bring at least some adults to the point of decision solely through methods that may be properly described as educational. There are, for instance, cases in which men are led to Christ through the cumulative influence of Christian wives or of intimate association with Christian friends or of the fellowship and instruction which they find in Bible classes. In such cases the consciences and the religious natures of those converted are gradually awakened until they are brought to a point where they realize their need of Christ and are willing to surrender their lives to him.

IV. DANGERS AND LIMITATIONS

Important as educational evangelism is, however, in building the kingdom of God, it is not without its dangers and its limitations.

1. It is always possible that a program of religious education may degenerate into mere mechanical

routine. Religion is not a matter of rules, but of life; not a matter of information, but of emotional attitude; not a matter of ceremonial observances, but of immediate fellowship with God. It is possible diligently to instruct a child in rules of conduct, to impart to him a vast fund of information about the Bible, and to train him in the rigid observance of form and ritual, and yet leave him emotionally bankrupt and spiritually dead. In order that educational evangelism may be really effective, the whole process must be thoroughly vital and deeply spiritual—that is, it must be shot through with religious fervor, must provide adequate opportunity for the cultivation of the devotional life, and must so reveal Christ and his ideal as to awaken in the pupil a passionate response of love and trust and self-devotion. An educational process that falls short of this may be soundly ethical, but it is not religious, nor can it produce the spiritual fruits which are found in the characters of those who live in fellowship with God. Teachers of religion, therefore, need to be on their guard against falling into mere mechanical routine. Religious pedagogy is valuable only as a means of making religious truth so real and vital to pupils that it will become the great motivating power in their lives.

2. There are multitudes of men and women among us who are not beyond the reach of hope but who, nevertheless, as will be more fully explained in the next chapter, cannot be awakened and won to Christ by ordinary educational processes alone. In such cases the educational method must be supplemented by the

5   65

more intensive and dramatic appeal that is made through the revival.

SUGGESTIONS FOR STUDY

1. Explain the meaning of educational evangelism.

2. Upon what fundamental assumption does it proceed?

3. Explain the Augustinian view of human nature and show that it is contrary (a) to the fundamental teachings of the Bible, (b) to the historic position of Methodism, and (c) to the observed facts of human life.

4. Explain why our great evangelistic opportunity is with childhood.

5. Discuss the dangers and limitations of educational evangelism.

6. What do these suggest to you?

66

CHAPTER V

[EVANGELISTIC METHODS (CONTINUED)

I. Uses of the Revival

ANOTHER important method of evangelism is the revival. There are two common types of revivals—namely, the general and the local revival.

1. The general revival, which is often national and sometimes even international in its scope, while it requires human coöperation, is not, as a rule, the result of human prevision and planning, but of great providential events and movements for which human planning is only indirectly responsible. All down through the history of the Church there have been times when, through some unusual succession of occurrences or combination of forces, God has moved upon the Church with extraordinary potency, quickening its spiritual life and setting in motion great tides of spiritual influence that have swept out beyond ecclesiastical boundaries and brought about an awakening of the religious interest of multitudes who were not connected with any kind of religious organization. Such revivals, though immensely important, cannot, in the very nature of the case, be assigned a definite place in the regular program of the Church. All that the Church can do is to pray that the way may be opened for their coming and then watch for the signs of their approach, making sure that she is ready for the providential occasion when it arrives. It will be

readily seen that a study of revivals of this kind would be out of place in a course like that on which we are engaged.

2. Local revivals, on the other hand, are generally the direct outcome of intelligently and deliberately planned efforts to accomplish certain definite results in the life of the community which cannot be accomplished by normal educational processes.

(1) Under the conditions which at present exist in the Church and in society, it is inevitable that many will come to manhood and womanhood without becoming Christians and that some of those who started in the way of life in childhood will yield to the allurements of the world and fall away from their first love. The Church must not despair of men and women of either of these classes. On the contrary, she is in duty bound to do everything that it is possible for her to do to save them. But, since they have reached a period in life in which character has become more or less fixed and ways of thought and conduct have hardened in habits, it is often impossible either to reach them effectively through educational agencies alone or to move them by ordinary methods of appeal. Many such, however, may still be awakened and won to Christ through the influence of the intensive method of evangelism commonly known as the revival.

I read many years ago a striking illustration of what I mean in a sermon by Henry Ward Beecher. He said that when he was a boy in New England lumbermen used to go into the hills in winter and cut down trees, saw them into logs, drag them down to the frozen streams, bind them into rafts, and leave them on the ice, where they would lie undisturbed for several months. But when the warm days of spring came, melting the ice and snow and sending great volumes of water down into the valleys, these rafts would be lifted out of their winter moorings and floated on the currents of the swollen streams down to the seaports, there to be transformed into lumber for the building of cities. So in every community, he says, there are always men and women, young and middle-aged and old, who are so bound by worldliness and evil habits that it requires the white heat of a great religious awakening to melt their icy fetters and release those flood tides of spiritual life and power that are required to sweep them into the kingdom of God.

(2) It is difficult, if not impossible, however, for the ordinary Christian community to maintain continuously the kind of united, concentrated, and intensive effort which the revival requires. The average Church member is a very busy person. For most of our very best and most faithful Christians are breadwinners or home-keepers and are necessarily burdened with many cares and with much serving. The very physical limitations under which they labor, therefore, make it impossible for them to give more than a limited portion of their time to evangelistic work and render it exceedingly difficult for them continuously to maintain that high degree of spiritual fervor which is an essential factor in the successful revival. A group of Christians, therefore, agree for a limited period to give more time and more concentrated attention to evangelistic effort than it is

69

possible for them to give continuously. They meet together frequently for prayer and conference. They plan the work which they are to undertake and take counsel with one another about the best ways of doing it, and they curtail their hours of rest and in some cases temporarily neglect their ordinary business in order that they may devote themselves completely to the task in hand. Meanwhile the minister, having made a careful study of the local situation, seeks by means of fervid messages that are adapted to their needs to reach and arouse and win those who are brought to the services through the personal efforts of his fellow workers.

The revival is not an effort to induce an indifferent God to pay an occasional visit to a congregation or a community from which he is ordinarily separated or a reluctant God to do something which he does not greatly desire to do. God is always at hand and always ready to share his life in overflowing measure with those who are ready to receive it. But for the accomplishment of spiritual results he must work mainly through human beings, and the revival is simply an occasion when a group of consecrated Christian people devote themselves for a season more completely to a certain type of service than is continuously possible for them.

(3) It is sometimes said that the ideal at which the Church should aim is a revival that continues the year round. Such an ideal, however, under our common human conditions, is impossible of realization. Every Church ought certainly to be spiritually alive and active in evangelistic work the year round, but the very idea

70

of the revival is that of securing unusual spiritual results by such a concentration of attention and energy on a certain type of service as cannot be kept up all the time.

3. A careful study of the foregoing paragraph will naturally suggest that, besides its purpose to arrest and awaken and win the unconverted to Christ, the revival has a distinct educational value and should be regarded as an important factor in the educational program of the Church. Notice what is said about the heavy demands that are made upon the time and thought and energy of the average Christian by the ordinary routine of his daily duties as breadwinner or home-keeper and about the multitudinous distractions that grow out of his business and his social relations. Recall the further fact that many of his contacts are with people whose influence is by no means friendly to the development of his moral and spiritual life, and it at once becomes apparent that most Christians will inevitably find themselves engaged in a constant struggle against a tendency to fall into a condition of spiritual lethargy and to adopt an attitude of moral compromise.

The revival not only brings temporary release from these burdens and distractions and from the temptation to grow weary in well doing, but it also sets in motion influences that reinvigorate our spiritual life, rekindle our religious fervor, and send us back with renewed zeal and energy to the homely tasks of everyday life. Every Christian needs occasionally a special season of spiritual recuperation. There are some who find opportunity for such recuperation in the summer gatherings for Christian fellowship and religious study which have become so conspicuous a feature of the program of the modern Church. For the rank and file of Church members, however, such opportunity comes only through the annual revival.

II. LIMITATIONS OF THE REVIVAL

But the best things lend themselves most readily to abuse. We need not be surprised, therefore, to discover that the revival as well as the educational method of evangelism has its dangers and its limitations.

1. Almost every one knows something about what is popularly spoken of as crowd psychology, and that one of its characteristics is that almost any group of people, a community, a city, or even a whole nation, may be swept by a wave of emotion, often hysterical in its intensity, that has back of it no adequate reason for its existence. A familiar illustration is found in the account in the nineteenth chapter of the Acts of the mob at Ephesus which threatened the life of St. Paul. The people had been stirred to a frenzy by the shrewd maneuverings of a certain silversmith named Demetrius, who appealed at once to their cupidity and their religious fanaticism by suggesting that it was possible that the preaching of the apostle might seriously interfere with their business and at the same time bring discredit upon the worship of Diana. This suggestion was rapidly passed from mouth to mouth, until by and by practically the whole city was stirred to a frenzy of excitement, and the people rushed madly through the streets shouting: "Great is Diana of the Ephesians!"

72

Most of them, however, did not know what it was all about: "Some cried one thing and some another: for the assembly was in confusion; and the most part knew not wherefore they were come together." They had simply become the victims of a sudden tempest of mob frenzy and were ready for any crime that their leaders might suggest. Illustrations of the same manifestation, more familiar and nearer at home, may be seen in such occurrences as the real estate booms which a few years ago drove many of our American cities into orgies of wild and extravagant speculation.

(1) These illustrations are given, not for the purpose of discrediting revivals, but only for the purpose of pointing out one of the dangers to which they are subject. At certain times and in certain types of communities conditions arise which make it comparatively easy for a forceful and magnetic leader to start a wave of religious emotion that has no background of vital conviction or sound teaching. There is always danger that a so-called revival may assume this type, and the danger is made all the greater by the fact that the revivalist himself may not be a conscious charlatan. There doubtless have occasionally been bad men who took advantage of the readiness of human nature to yield to certain kinds of emotional appeal in order to glorify themselves and incidentally to replenish their purses. I am persuaded, however, that such cases are exceptional. Spurious revivalism, in most instances, comes from the fact that the leaders themselves are deceived; they take shallow emotionalism that has no

real conviction back of it as a sign of a real work of grace in the community.

(2) The possibility of such abuses is not to be interpreted, however, as a reason for abandoning the use of the revival but, as has already been suggested, as simply a warning against one of the dangers to which it is liable. Every religious appeal is in some sense an appeal to the emotional nature, since religion is a matter of emotional attitude as well as of conviction. In the revival this emotional appeal reaches an unusual degree of intensity. Indeed, the fact that there are types of people who can be moved in no other way except through such appeal, as has already been pointed out, is one of the reasons why the revival is necessary. In order, however, that an appeal to adults or those who are approaching adulthood may have any moral or spiritual significance it must be an appeal to real conviction, and where such conviction does not exist it must be created by definite instruction given either from the pulpit or in some other legitimate way. It is of no avail to call on a man to surrender his life to Christ who knows nothing about Christ or what he stands for or what it means to be his disciple. An adult's surrender to Christ is significant only in proportion as it is a voluntary response of the heart and the will to a real revelation of Christ and of the kind of life which he requires.

(3) This means, as has already been shown, that the revival itself, in order to be truly effective, must in some sense be educational. That is, the revivalist, as a basis for his invitation, must so interpret Christ and the

74

ideals for which he stands as to fill those to whom the invitation is extended with a loathing for their sinful and selfish lives and a passionate longing to arise from the lethargy into which they have fallen and to live as Christ would have them live. This is necessary even in the cases of adults who had some measure of religious training in childhood, but later fell into evil ways or became so absorbed in material concerns that they lost whatever religious interest they may once have had. For such men and women will, as a rule, be found to have in their minds only meager and vague ideas in regard to the personality and work and teachings of Christ, and therefore the only way of effective approach to them is by a process of teaching, either in the Church school or from the pulpit, that will give form and substance to their indefinite and chaotic notions.

(4) If the revival is thus properly prepared for and wisely and intelligently conducted, it is altogether possible that through it many may be reached and won who cannot be reached and won in any other way. For it must not be inferred from anything that has been said that group influence is always and necessarily bad. On the contrary, it may be and often is thoroughly wholesome, and its proper use in evangelistic effort, therefore, is entirely legitimate.

2. There are types of men and women who cannot be reached through revival methods. With some of these opposition may be a mere matter of prejudice growing out of abuses, either real or imaginary, of which they have been witnesses. In other cases, however, it is

75

the result of some personal peculiarity such as a tendency to excessive reticence in regard to the deeper experiences of their lives or an instinctive fear of becoming the victims of mere group emotion. In all of these cases it is our duty as Christian evangelists to take men as we find them and to seek to reach them by such means as are likely to prove most effective. In other words, instead of insisting on dealing with men and women as if they were all cast in precisely the same mold, we should recognize their temperamental differences and follow St. Paul's principle of seeking to become all things to all men if by any means we may win them.

3. The conditions of modern life are much less favorable to the revival than were those of the simpler and less strenuous days of our fathers. We live in an age of big business and big cities and of steam and electricity and crashing machinery. The tumult of the world is continually in our ears and the glamour of the world in our eyes. The bewildering complexity of life, with its multitudinous distractions and engagements, leaves us with but little time for repose and quiet thinking. We are absorbed in getting and spending, in hurrying hither and thither on errands of business or pleasure, in seeking new sensations and launching new enterprises. It is inevitable that it should be found increasingly difficult at such a time to turn the attention of those who have been caught in this mad rush to religion. That we actually find it so is made manifest by the sensational methods to which we too often resort to attract the outside multitudes to our

76

revival services. Such methods, however, even conceding their legitimacy, are sure to prove but temporarily effective; for not even the genius of the most original evangelist is equal to the task of satisfying the demands of the seeker after the sensational for new excitements. Methods that attract this year will have grown stale and lost their drawing power a year or two hence, and something still more spectacular will be required to excite the jaded nerves of the habitual seeker after something new and sensational.

And so it grows ever more difficult to reach through any kind of legitimate evangelistic appeal those who have already become absorbed in the cares of business or professional life or in the feverish quest for pleasure.

All of these considerations lead directly to one conclusion—namely, that it is the imperative duty of the Church, instead of waiting until men have become blighted and hardened by sin or fixed in their prejudices and habits or absorbed in the mad chase after money or excitement, to take advantage of the opportunity for making disciples that is found in the freedom and plasticity and open-mindedness of childhood. For this opportunity, when once it is gone, never returns, and no efforts that we may put forth in after years can compensate for our failure to make the most of it.

4. The methods which the revival employs are not only unnecessary in the case of children, but are entirely unsuited to them. While the child is the victim of an inheritance of evil tendencies, he is not a sinner in the sense in which an adult may be a sinner. He has not purposely chosen the way of rebellion against

77

God, nor has he formed any fixed evil habits. On the contrary, his spiritual nature is plastic and responsive. He needs, therefore, no cyclone to arouse him from spiritual lethargy. The close personal influence of Christian parents and teachers, recruited and made effective by a genial atmosphere of love and reverence in the home and the church, is sufficient for his religious and moral awakening. Indeed, the kind of intense emotional appeal that is often found necessary in the revival, instead of helping him, may prove really hurtful to him. For the feelings of the young are easily touched, and any kind of intense emotional pressure may result in reactions so violent as to produce permanent injury to the nervous system. To the influences of such unusual excitements are due most of the peculiar fears that so often haunt the lives of little children and that in many cases prove a serious hindrance to their healthy and harmonious development. It is unwise, therefore, since children may be so easily awakened and won to a saving faith in Christ by normal and wholesome educational methods, to take the needless risk of subjecting them to the intense emotional appeal of the revival.

5. Another limitation of the revival method of evangelism grows out of the fact that it is necessarily periodical. Evangelism in the largest sense means the process of making Christians, and one of the essential steps in this process is the bringing of each individual into a vital, personal relation with Jesus Christ. Christian experience must have a beginning, but it must also have a continuous growth. We all

78

begin the Christian life as babes in Christ; but the ideal which St. Paul sets before us is that we shall "all attain unto the unity of the faith, and of the knowledge of the Son of God, unto a full grown man, unto the measure of the stature of the fullness of Christ." (Eph. 4: 13.) That is, the making of a Christian is not a process that comes to an end when an individual has been led to accept Christ, but is to continue until he has attained unto the full maturity of Christian life and experience.

Now the revival affords in many cases an effective means for leading people to enter definitely upon the Christian life, but it does not provide the conditions of normal and continuous religious development. It must be followed, therefore, by an adapted educational process if its results are to be permanent. The history of the Church is filled with the record of spiritual tragedies that have followed revivals because no adequate provision was made for carrying to completion the work which these revivals began.

III. Evaluation

The conclusions to which this study leads us may be summarized as follows:

The Church should seek to carry out a complete evangelistic program and to this end should make the most effective use of all available agencies and all legitimate methods, giving to each its rightful place and its due proportion of emphasis. A Church that does not avail itself of the opportunity furnished by the revival, besides failing to win many who are not to be regarded as entirely inaccessible to the religious appeal, will run the risk of falling into formalism and spiritual lethargy. A Church, on the other hand, that depends mainly on revivals will fail not only to make the most of the wonderful evangelistic opportunity that is furnished by childhood and youth, but also to develop those whom it succeeds in bringing to Christ into vigorous and efficient Christians. Every congregation should seek through occasional special revival efforts both to quicken its own spiritual life and to win those who cannot be won in any other way. But every congregation should also be a center of continuous and intelligently directed educational evangelism. And, as between these methods, it is easy to see where the leading emphasis should be placed. The chief field of evangelistic opportunity is that of childhood, and the only evangelistic method that is applicable in this field is the educational method. Instead, therefore, of attempting to make the revival a substitute for educational evangelism, we should regard it as supplementary to it

IV. The Place of the Church School.

1. In order that the Church may carry out a complete evangelistic program, giving to educational evangelism its rightful place of primacy, it must have a definite educational policy both for the whole body and for each local congregation. That is, it must have an organized system of Church schools and a carefully wrought out plan for equipping these schools for effective work. Such a plan will include, among other things, provision for promoting the erection of adequate

buildings, for the training of officers and teachers, for the production of a thoroughly adapted curriculum, for the creation of a unified organization and program in the local congregation, and for the development of such an educational consciousness in the membership of the Church as would insure its hearty and intelligent support.

It requires but a limited knowledge of the situation that at present exists in the Methodist Episcopal Church, South, to enable one to see that it falls far short of the ideal thus briefly outlined.

There has been during recent years a marvelous increase of interest throughout the Church in religious education, but we have not yet reached the point of giving it a central place in our evangelistic work. Indeed, many of us have not yet come to think of evangelism at all in terms of an educational process. We think of it rather as identical with revivalism and do not give serious consideration to any other type of evangelistic effort except the revival. As a result of this attitude many of our Sunday school teachers do not regard their work as having any direct relation to evangelism and hence have no definite evangelistic aim.

And great as has been the recent development of our Sunday school work, we are still far from anything approaching a unified and comprehensive system of religious education. On the contrary, we have in each congregation a number of organizations taking part in the educational task without any effort at correlation and coördination. Such an arrangement inevitably results in confusion and overlapping and makes im-

6   81

possible the development of any clear-cut educational program with a definite aim and a definite plan for accomplishing this aim. We shall never be able to do the most effective work in educational evangelism until we rid ourselves of this confusion. What we need is one Church School in each congregation charged with all the various phases of religious education and clearly conscious of the nature and meaning of its evangelistic mission.

2. The advantages of such a school as an agency in evangelism are apparent:

It would concentrate the attention of all of the educational forces of the Church upon the task of educational evangelism.

It would tend to develop an ever-increasing multitude of active and efficient lay evangelists and an evangelistic program that would be continuous throughout the entire year.

And these lay evangelists would have the advantage of immediate and vital personal contact with those whom they sought to bring into the kingdom and of being able to adapt both their methods and their teaching material to people of all ages and stages of development.

SUGGESTIONS FOR STUDY

1. Explain two types of revivals.
2. Are revivals likely to have a permanent place in the evangelistic program of the Church? Why?
3. What educational value has the revival?
4. Explain the chief danger of the revival.

82

5. Have illustrations of this danger come under your personal observation?

6. How is this danger to be guarded against?

7. Have you known types of people who could not be reached successfully through the revival?

8. Are conditions at present more or less favorable for reach-' ing outsiders through revivals than they formerly were? Give reasons for your answer.

9. What would you regard as a complete evangelistic program for a local Church?

83

CHAPTER VI

EARLY CHILDHOOD

SINCE we are dealing primarily with evangelism in the Sunday school, and since the Sunday school is an educational agency, our main interest in these studies is naturally in educational evangelism. And if the conclusions in regard to child nature which are stated in the preceding chapters are accepted, it follows as a necessary consequence that the evangelistic process should begin with the beginning of the child's life.

I. EVANGELISM AS APPLIED TO EARLY CHILDHOOD

1. While the newly born babe is neither religious nor moral, he is potentially both a religious and a moral being. That is, he is endowed with religious and moral capacities which may be awakened and developed and through the development of which he may be brought into a vital personal relation with Jesus Christ. And this is what evangelism means as applied to the little child. The process should begin with the beginning of his life. "Genuine and true, living religion," says Froebel, "reliable in danger and struggles, in times of oppression and need, in joy and pleasure, must come to man in his infancy. . . . The religious spirit, a fervid life in God and with God, in all conditions and circumstances, will hardly, in later years, rise to full vigorous life, if it has not grown up with man from his infancy. On the other hand, a religious spirit thus

84

fostered and nursed from early infancy will rise supreme in all storms and dangers of life." In other words, he maintains that the realization of the full possibilities of each stage of development "depends on the vigorous, complete, and characteristic development of each and all preceding stages of life." This means that in the matter of religious education the first years of the child's life are supremely important and that the child who is denied proper nurture and training during these years loses something for which no subsequent effort can make up. He may be awakened and converted later on, but it will be exceedingly difficult for him to attain that inner harmony and that complete sense of being at home with God which would have been possible to him if from the beginning he had been "brought up in the nurture and admonition of the Lord."

2. It follows from the above that the first school of evangelism, both in time and importance, is the home and that to no other class of builders of the kingdom does there come such an opportunity for making disciples as that which is given to Christian fathers and mothers. The influence of their personalities and bearing and the general atmosphere that pervades the home begin to influence the life of the child a few hours after birth, and for a number of years they continue to be, not only the most important, but almost the sole factors in determining his development. Mrs. Mumford, in "The Dawn of Religion in the Mind of the Child," after calling attention to the fact that it is as a result of the slow and unconscious sifting out of repeated experiences brought about by the things done

85

for him or before him that the child learns about the world around him and the world within him, adds:

Is it not clear, then, that, from the first, there must be a difference between the growth of the child's knowledge of God and his knowledge of other matters—a difference more marked, according to the child's natural responsiveness and according to his native spiritual endowment? For when his mother *prays*, her attitude, her tone of voice, her expression of face, the very touch of her hand, are different from what they are at any other time and under any other circumstances; and to this difference the child instinctively responds. Silently and unconsciously, *her* reverence, *her* love, communicated to him, in some strange and exquisite way, along the chords of common sympathy, call forth in him, almost from the first, feelings akin to her own. What she feels, he too begins to feel: and a child is capable of religious feeling long before he is capable of religious thought.

These remarks at once suggest the possibility of greatly increasing the effectiveness of the agencies through which the child's religious life is awakened by intelligent and purposeful effort. Froebel, for instance, suggests that the mother should frequently pray by the bedside of her babe with hands folded and eyes uplifted and that she should soothe him to sleep in the evening and awaken him in the morning by softly singing simple religious songs to him.

The writer, a number of years ago, heard a cultivated Christian woman say that she began in a definite and purposeful way the religious education of her first baby as soon as she was able to sit up and hold the baby in her arms. Upon being asked how she went about this sacred task, she replied that she began by singing simple religious songs and then, with eyes uplifted to heaven, uttering a few simple sentences of prayer for the divine blessing. Later she began to talk to the child about the love and goodness of God and the precious gifts through which this love and goodness are expressed. At first, of course, the little one understood nothing of all that her mother said and did, but as the process was continued from day to day there was a gradual awakening of both her intellectual and spiritual nature and an increasing response both of mind and heart. As the child grew older the educational process was of course modified to meet the demands of her unfolding life. The field of her knowledge and interest was gradually widened, and she was taught to express through appropriate words and actions the love and reverence that were gradually awakened within her. And so she was led step by step into a deeper experience of the religious life and a more real fellowship with the heavenly Father.

And it must be kept constantly in mind that this is to be the aim of evangelism in the case of the little child just as it is in the case of one who is more advanced in life. "Merely to tell a child about God," says Mrs. Mumford in the volume quoted above, "and then to teach him a simple form of prayer is but a poor substitute for teaching him *to know* God. Secondhand knowledge can never be a sufficient basis of intercourse. Love is the necessary basis for prayer if it is to be real." The spirit of love and reverence must be first awakened in the mind of the child through the atmosphere of the home and the religious life of the father and mother expressing itself in song, in attitudes and words of worship, and in daily acts of service. And then, when the child is old enough to understand, this love and reverence must by definite instruction be lifted up to God. That is, the parents must tell the child about the loving Father to whom they are able to speak about all their joys and troubles and to whom both they and he are indebted for all the good gifts of life. This instruction must, of course, be largely concrete. That is, it must be in the form of stories showing God's love and goodness and power and of illustrations drawn from nature and from the child's everyday experiences.

Through such teaching the child gradually becomes conscious of the presence of the Unseen Friend and is made ready for entering into personal communion with him. Prayer in the form of both petition and thanksgiving becomes natural to him, and, although his understanding is very meager, he begins to have real and vital fellowship with the heavenly Father. And this is the beginning of all spiritual attainment. Potentially everything is involved in this experience that belongs to the experiences of later life. The child becomes a partaker of the divine nature in precisely the same sense in which one who is brought to a knowledge of God in adult life does so.

3. The question is often raised at this point as to whether or not a child thus brought up needs to be regenerated. To be sure he does. Regeneration is the cleansing and quickening of the human life through personal touch with the life of God. And this cleansing and quickening can be brought about in no other way.

"Except one be born from above," says Jesus, "he cannot see the kingdom of God." When I was a lad on the farm I discovered that the most lusty stalk of corn standing alone in the middle of a cotton field never bore more than a few grains of fruit. Later I learned the reason why this was so. Each embryonic grain in the ear had to be fertilized by the pollen falling from the tassels, and since one tassel did not furnish a sufficiency of pollen the single stalk was doomed to practical barrenness. So each soul must be purified and its spiritual potentialities must be recruited by the indwelling of the Holy Spirit, by the birth from above. Were it otherwise, it is possible to conceive that one might come to the fullness of spiritual life without the help of religion.

4. This does not mean, however, that the child must pass through a religious crisis similar to that through which an older person who has wandered away from God often passes in turning away from his sinful ways and coming back to the Father's house. In our common speech we use the word "conversion" as synonymous with "regeneration," and there is no objection to our doing so provided we keep in mind the fact that it is never so used in the New Testament. In the King James Version the verb "to convert" or "to be converted" occurs only a few times (Matthew 13: 15; Mark 4: 12; John 12: 40; Acts 28: 27; Matthew 18: 3; Luke 22: 32; Acts 3: 19; James 5: 19, 20), and in every case it means to "turn" or "turn about." In other words, it always refers to a purely human act, while regeneration is an act of the Holy Spirit. For

89

instance, when James says, "If any among you err from the truth, and one convert him," he does not mean "if one regenerate him," but "if one cause him to turn about and face toward God."

It does not follow, therefore, that, because every one must be regenerated, every one must be converted. On the contrary, many children are brought into true fellowship with God and receive the quickening of the Holy Spirit long before they are old enough to enter definitely upon a life of sin. In other words, they learn to love and trust God in the same way and at the same time that they learn to love and trust their mothers, and, while they may often fail in duty just as older Christians do, they no more think about renouncing their loyalty to him than they do about renouncing their loyalty to their parents. A story is told of a Christian woman who went to a little girl during a revival service and asked her if she would not come to Jesus. The little child replied in her naïve and simple way: "I have never gone away from him yet." That may have been literally true, and it may be as true of a fifteen-year-old girl as of an eight-year-old girl. Dr. George H. Betts, a few years ago, sent to a large number of active Christian workers the following questions:

(1) Can you point to *some particular time or occasion* when you began the Christian life, in the act commonly known as *conversion*, meaning by this *a turning from a state of spiritual coldness and indifference or rebellion* to a recognition of the claims of Christ upon you and a consciousness of his acceptance of you?

(2) Did you *grow so gradually* into your present religious status that you *cannot point to any particular time or occasion* when you were *converted* and began the Christian life?

About forty-five per cent of those who replied to these questions answered that they had experienced definite conversion, while about fifty-five per cent said that they could fix no time or place of conversion, but from their earliest recollection they had counted themselves as Christians, having been brought up in Christian homes and under religious instruction. Testimonies of similar import are so numerous as to leave no doubt of the fact that many children come under the regenerating power of the Holy Spirit at a very early period in their lives and never become deliberate rebels against God. The fact that such children cannot point to the particular time when this experience began does not in the least discredit its reality and genuineness. One of the most important facts in the lives of most of us is our love for our mothers. We should no more think of questioning this love than we should think of questioning our existence. Of course we know that this love had a beginning, for there was a time when we did not love at all, but how and when the vital bond that unites us with our mothers came into existence is a matter about which we shall forever remain in ignorance. And so it may be in regard to the bond of faith and love that unites us with Jesus Christ. If we are sure that we are his and he is ours, we need not trouble ourselves because we cannot remember when this sacred relation was established.

5. The clear meaning of all this is that it is possible for the Holy Spirit to reach the heart of the little child and for the little child to have a true religious experience.

(1) This view is in accord with the teaching of the holy Scriptures. According to the Gospel of Luke, the angel who announced to Zacharias the birth of John the Baptist declared that he should be filled with the Holy Spirit even from his mother's womb. (Luke 1: 15.) St. Paul exhorts fathers to bring their children up "in the nurture and admonition of the Lord" (Eph. 6: 4), and to Timothy he writes, "From a babe thou hast known the sacred writings, which are able to make thee wise unto salvation through faith which is in Christ Jesus" (2 Tim. 3: 15). Dr. Trumbull tells us that with their background of Jewish training the disciples to whom Jesus gave the Great Commission could not have understood it otherwise than as a command to go and make disciples by the process of Christian training; and it is certain that the facts of Jewish history are favorable to this interpretation.

(2) The view which I am here maintaining, in the second place, is in accord with reason. We know now as never before that from the viewpoint of determining character and destiny the first years in the life of a human being are by all odds the most significant and important. It is in this period that the mind of the child is most plastic and impressionable. The atmosphere in which he lives and the training which he receives during these years determine the whole trend of his future life. It is inconceivable, therefore, that the heavenly Father has so arranged matters that he cannot come into vital touch with a living soul at the very time when his vitalizing power is most needed and will count for most in determining that soul's development.

92

(3) This view is further confirmed by the study of our own experiences and by our actual observations of child life. There are many men and women who know that at the point of their earliest recollection they had already entered upon a definite life of faith. And what Christian is there to-day who is not acquainted with little children who show every evidence of a truly vital religious experience?

Take, for instance, the following illustrations: A lad six years of age dictated a letter to his grandmother in which he told her about two stanzas of poetry which he had recently learned. "I got a little notion," he said, "that I was afraid to go to bed in the dark, and so mother taught me these poems"; and then he quoted the following stanzas from Tennyson and Whittier; "Closer is he than breathing, and nearer than hands and feet," and

> I know not where his islands lift
> Their fronded palms in air;
> I only know I cannot drift
> Beyond his love and care.

And after explaining that the stanzas referred to Jesus, he added, "I like those poems. Somehow they make me feel good in the dark." The same lad said to his mother one day: "Mother, I think it so much fun to pray. When I shut my eyes and everybody gets quiet, it seems that nobody is there but God and me." That this experience was not only real but had a definite ethical content is indicated by the reaction of the same child after his mother had read to him a book on the life of Paul. He had been intensely interested in the story from beginning to end, and when the entire volume of something like two hundred and fifty pages had been finished he said to her: "Mother, I want to grow up to be a brave, good man like St. Paul and to help people just as he helped them. Do you think God will let me?" Of course this particular child has had unusually careful religious training. I am quite sure, however, that his case is by no means exceptional and that it furnishes unquestionable evidence of the fact that a little child may have a vital Christian experience.

6. The position which I am here maintaining is not something new in Methodism, but has been held by our Methodist fathers from the very beginning, as the following quotations will show:

Dr. Richard Watson, one of the great theologians of early Methodism: "We are bound to conclude that the kingdom of heaven in some sense is composed of them (little children). They are its subjects and partakers of its blessings; and if they are the subjects of his spiritual kingdom on earth, then, until the moment that by actual sin they bring personal condemnation upon themselves, they remain heirs of the kingdom of eternal glory; and if they become subjects of the latter dying, then a precious vital relation must have existed on earth between them and Christ, their Redeemer and Sanctifier."

Dr. Stephen G. Olin, one of the honored leaders of American Methodism in the middle of the nineteenth century: "We believe that God renews those infants who die and go to heaven before they know how to discern the right hand from the left. This quite dissolves the philosophical objection; there is no natural obstacle to the work of grace in a child."

Dr. W. P. Harrison, a prominent theologian of Southern Methodism half a century ago, in "The Living Christ," issued by our Publishing House: "God does not leave the soul of any little child to the unquestioned dominion and power of Satan. Under the laws of thought within the environments which are as various as the conditions which control the physical development of man the soul and its Redeemer meet; and, whatever may be the record of manhood or the issues of old age, the little child is placed, by the mercy of God, under the protecting shield of the Second Adam."

In a little book entitled "Christian Cradlehood," by Dr. Richard Abbey, of the Mississippi Conference, issued by our Publishing House in 1881, we find the following striking passage: "I know of no natural reason why a child may not feel divine love as early as he is capable of feeling parental love. He is unable to define or understand it. It is a felt satisfaction of being good. This consciousness of doing right and of meeting approval is a very early development and is what we mean in later years by 'enjoying religion.' There is nothing in either nature or grace that inhibits its early beginning. Natural depravity appertains no more to cradle life than to youth or manhood. It is simply universal. The grace of Christ meets it in the cradle precisely as it does in maturer years. There is no more of a necessary sinful period somewhere in the first five or ten years than in later years."

95

II. The Religion of Early Childhood

The religion of the little child is just as real as that of the adult, and yet it differs from that of the adult as childhood differs from adulthood. "When I was a child," says St. Paul, "I spake as a child, I felt as a child, I thought as a child." (1 Cor. 13: 11.) He could not have spoken and felt and thought in any other way. It is a serious mistake for us to attempt to impose our adult experiences upon little children. Rather should we permit them, religiously and otherwise, to live out their own lives as children, understanding that it is by so doing that they are to prepare for the later experiences of youth, of young manhood and womanhood, and of adulthood.

1. The child's religion is not a matter of intellectual conviction reached through a process of reasoning, but rather the upspringing of the heart to meet the appeal of Jesus Christ as he is revealed in the lives and through the teachings of those whom the child loves and trusts. It will be a long time before the metaphysical and theological questions about which older people concern themselves will trouble him. Meanwhile, however, if he is kept under proper influences and in a proper environment, his love for Christ and his loyalty to Christ will remain just as real and vital as those of people of maturer years.

2. It would be unreasonable, however, to expect in the faith of the little child the vigor and stability that ought to characterize the faith of the adult Christian. A few years ago I decided that, instead of buying plants

in the spring for my garden, I would raise them myself.
So I prepared the soil in boxes, put them in a warm
nook in the basement of my residence, and planted the
seeds of such vegetables and flowers as I wished to
cultivate. In due time the seeds sprang up and the
little plants were green and beautiful. I failed to
realize, however, how delicate they were and how necessary it was that I should give them constant and proper
attention. And so, it chancing one week that I was
unusually busy, I neglected them for two or three days
and, as a consequence, when I returned, found that
every one of them had died. In the matter of tender-
ness and delicacy the religious life of the little child
may very well be compared with the life of those young
plants. The plants would have soon grown into lusty
stalks if they had been watered and fed and kept in a
properly ventilated atmosphere. And so the spiritual
life of the child will flourish and grow if it has the right
kind of environment and the right kind of nurture and
training, but without these it will soon weaken and die.
The lad of three or four who is so devoted to his mother
that he cannot bear to be absent from her for an hour
would probably forget her altogether if she were to
leave him for half a year. All of which means that we
are not to content ourselves with mere beginnings, but
that through the continuous employment of the educational agencies previously described and the progressive adaptation of these agencies to the unfolding life we
are to seek to enable the child to grow as the Master
grew—"in wisdom and stature and in favor with God
and man."

7   97

III. The Part of the Sunday School

What part has the Sunday school in the evangelization of the little child?

1. In almost every class of beginners or primaries will be found children whose religious nurture and training have been so neglected that it will be necessary for the teacher to begin at the very beginning. That is, it will be necessary for her in the case of each child to seek to make up for the failure of the home by endeavoring through an intelligently directed educational process to awaken his religious nature and bring him into personal fellowship with the heavenly Father. Of course the opportunities which the Sunday school affords for accomplishing this are not to be compared with those offered in the home. And yet the trained and consecrated teacher, by a wise and diligent use of the limited time and opportunities at her command, may influence in a vital and permanent way the plastic young lives committed to her. For suggestions as to methods teachers are referred to properly accredited books dealing with the nurture and training of children in the beginners and primary departments. It may be remarked in passing, however, that the same general principles which apply to the religious awakening of the child in the home apply also in the Sunday school.

2. Even in the case of the child who has received wise and careful religious training in the home, it is possible for the Sunday school effectively to supplement the work of the parents. For, besides the fact that the influence of the personality and work of the teacher,

whatever it may be, is just that much added to the training given in the home, is the fact that the school affords opportunities for widening the scope of the educational program. It affords opportunities, for instance, for group worship, for the development of group interests, and for teaching the child how to live with others, thus making it possible to begin to socialize his religion and to prepare him for taking his place in both Church and State. It is through the Sunday school that the child gets his first idea of the Church and of his broader social relationships.

It thus appears that there are vast multitudes of little children who must be introduced to Christ by the Church if they are to know him at all, and that the Church may have a very important part in the religious development even of children whose homes are positively and vitally Christian.

3. It is evidently especially important that the teachers of beginners and primaries shall keep in close touch with the homes of their pupils and that they shall secure the intelligent coöperation of their parents. This will require, in many cases, that while they are seeking to educate the pupils they must seek also to educate their fathers and mothers. And this will often mean awakening them to an adequate sense of their responsibility for the religious training of their children as well as helping them to prepare themselves for it.

IV. The Little Child and the Church

When it comes to the question of the relation of the little child to the Church, it must be confessed that the

Methodist Episcopal Church, South, has no clearly defined policy. In the Ritual for the Baptism of Infants, parts of which I have quoted in a previous chapter, it seems to be assumed that the baptized child is a member of the Church. For instance, the congregation is exhorted to pray that the child "may ever remain in the fellowship of God's holy Church"; and in the succeeding prayer, which the minister is required to use, there is a petition that the child "may abide safe in the ark of Christ's holy Church," and another that "he may ever remain in the number of God's faithful and elect children." As a matter of fact, however, baptized children are not counted as members of the Church, nor is any systematic effort made to keep a record of such children and to provide for their religious training.

That this is a much more serious matter than appears on the surface will become at once apparent when we come to consider what consequences may flow from it. Think, for instance, what effect it may have upon the life of a little child who goes regularly to church and Sunday school with his parents, and who has always thought of himself as identified with them in every interest of life, to be told that in the matter that he regards as of supreme concern to them he has no part nor lot. I have heard of many instances in which little children who were growing up in religious homes were bewildered and troubled upon discovering that they did not belong to the Church. There are two possible reactions from such a discovery. The child may decide that, because he is outside of the fellowship to which his parents belong and is not yet old enough and intelligent enough to get into this fellowship, he will entirely dismiss the matter as something that does not concern him. Perhaps it is in this way that the indifference of many children to the Church begins. On the other hand the child may insist on being formally received into the Church, and, if so, I think his desire should be granted, although it seems a pity that some way cannot be devised for giving little children their rightful place in the Church until they are old enough intelligently to take the vows of membership.

SUGGESTIONS FOR STUDY

1. What kind of being is the newly born babe?

2. Why should the home be the first school of evangelism?

3. Is it possible for a little child to be born from above? Explain your answer.

4. Explain the difference between conversion and regeneration.

5. Need a child know when the process of his spiritual quickening begins?

6. Give the result of your personal observation of the religion of childhood.

7. What is the historic teaching of Methodism as to the religious possibilities of early childhood?

8. What are the characteristics of the little child's religion?

9. What part has the Sunday school in the evangelism of the little child?

10. Discuss the relation of the little child to the Church.

101

CHAPTER VII

LATER CHILDHOOD

By later childhood I mean the period between the ages of nine and twelve. In this group there will be in most Sunday schools two general types, although each type will, of course, include several varieties.

1. Group One will be composed of boys and girls who have been brought up in the nurture and admonition of the Lord and who have already definitely entered upon the life of faith. Some of these will already have joined the Church. Others, while never having thought of themselves otherwise than as Christians, will not yet have raised the question of Church membership, either because their attention has not been definitely called to the matter or because they have regarded themselves as already in the Church. In the case of this group the problem of the junior worker is simply that of coöperating with the home in providing for the continuous normal development of a religious experience already begun. For of course all of these children will be found to have come from homes that are positively and vitally Christian.

2. Group Two will be composed of boys and girls whose religious education has been partially or totally neglected.

Since this course of lessons is designed primarily to furnish suggestions for initiating the Christian life rather than to give a comprehensive program of religious instruction and training, our first concern is with this second group.

I. DIFFICULTIES TO BE OVERCOME

In dealing with these children our first aim, as in all types of evangelism, will be to awaken the religious and moral nature of each child and to bring him into a vital personal relation through faith with Jesus Christ.

1. For a number of reasons the task will be found much more difficult than the religious awakening of the little child.

(1) The ready responsiveness which is so strikingly characteristic of the child of tender years has already greatly diminished.

(2) Perhaps there is no other period in the child's life in which it is more difficult for the adult to understand him than in the junior age. The adolescent is beginning, at any rate, to share the interests and the viewpoint of manhood or womanhood, but the junior's interests and viewpoint are all his own. A young girl who had an unusually vivid recollection of her later childhood said to the writer a few years ago: "When I was a child I found it impossible to understand grown-up people. When a particularly good thing came along, they never seemed to care anything about it; but they were always getting worked up over things that did not appear to me to be at all worth while." And I am quite willing to admit that the father, at least, of this particular girl was about as incapable of understanding her viewpoint as she was of understanding his. Perhaps

it is to the vague realization on the part of the child of this wide divergence in interest that we are to attribute the tendency to reticence which is so striking a characteristic of the junior, and especially of reticence in regard to his personal religious life. But whatever may be its cause, it increases immensely the junior worker's difficulty in making really vital approaches to her pupils.

(3) The junior child has much wider social contacts and a much wider range of interests than the beginner or primary possesses. He has his school, his clubs, and his circle of playmates, and is busily engaged in making all sorts of explorations into the strange and wonderful world in which he finds himself. Hence it is not nearly so easy to catch and hold his attention as it is to catch and hold the attention of the younger child.

(4) The difficulty is greatly increased by his physical vitality, with its accompanying restlessness and demand for activity. For the junior age is primarily an age of abounding physical life. "Some one," says Hartshorne in his "Childhood and Character," "has suggested how to get an idea of the exuberant abundance of life and energy in the years of later childhood. Think of how you'd feel some fine crisp morning, after a good night's rest, awake and ready for the day's work. Then multiply your feeling of strength and energy by ten. You are ten times as hungry, ten times as desirous of shouting and singing, ten times as good-natured, ten times as full of mischief, ten times as eager for the next act. That is the way a boy feels."

Of course it is exceedingly difficult for such a creature to sit still or to give continuous attention to any matter that does not call for his own active coöperation.

(5) In many cases the child of this age has already fallen under the influence of evil companions and definitely started in the wrong direction.

(6) The situation is still further complicated by the fact that in the case of children of this group teachers can count on but little help from parents. For if all homes were such as those from which the children of Group One are drawn, Group Two would be so small as to be practically negligible.

2. The following are some of the requisites for dealing successfully with boys and girls of this group.

(1) The teacher's own personality and character must be such as to command the respect and admiration of her pupils. This means, in the first place, that she must be true and open and sincere. There is no class of human beings that more readily detect or more heartily despise pretense of any kind than junior boys and girls.

The teacher must also unite in her character the elements of strength and beauty—that is, she must be able to deal with her pupils both tenderly and firmly. Any indication of indecision or of inability to maintain order and discipline is sure to forfeit their respect.

She must be cheerful, not cheerful simply in the sense that she forces herself to smile and say pleasant things, but cheerful in the sense in which one ought to be cheerful who draws her inspiration from daily fellowship with God and who looks at life through the eyes of faith. Junior children cannot be won by a religion that is somber and gloomy. They love sunlight and laughter and cheerful fellowship and cannot see why the worship of the heavenly Father should not add to the beauty and joyousness of life.

Finally, her love for her pupils must be so real and vital that she will not need to tell them about it, because it will express itself in the tones of her voice and in her whole manner and bearing toward them. The interest born of such love will do more than any course in psychology toward helping her to understand them, to establish relations of real vital friendship with them, and to find the easy passages to their hearts.

(2) The junior worker must be sure that her entire curriculum—the curriculum of instruction, the curriculum of worship, and the curriculum of activity—answers to the real needs of her pupils' lives.

For instance, the understanding of the average junior is still exceedingly limited and his interests entirely concrete. Abstract doctrines and general principles are beyond the range of his comprehension. He is not even concerned about heroism as an abstract quality. He is deeply interested, however, in particular heroes and their acts and hence will respond readily and enthusiastically to the appeal of the heroic Christ and of the hero stories of the Bible and the Christian Church. Of course it will be the aim of the teacher to enable her pupils to see the ugliness of sin and to despise it and turn from it with loathing. But the method should, in the main, be positive rather than negative. That is, the spiritual vision of the children should be

106

increased and their consciences quickened by such a progressive revelation of Christ and his ideal as will call forth their admiration and love and trust, and in proportion as this is accomplished the ugliness of sin will become apparent to them. For the ugliness of sin becomes apparent to one only through comparison with the beauty of holiness.

Juniors are not so lacking as they sometimes appear in the spirit of worship. But because of the restlessness due to their overflowing physical energy and of the fact that their minds are mainly occupied with the external world, services of worship must necessarily be brief and varied, moving forward without needless lagging and interruption, and they should be so planned as to enable the pupils, as far as possible, to participate in them.

Likewise the activities that are provided for them should be directed to the accomplishment of ends that appeal to their normal interests.

(3) All this implies that the successful teacher of juniors must know her pupils and be able to see from their viewpoint and to enter sympathetically into their lives. No one should undertake to work with juniors who has not carefully studied one or more such books as "A Study of the Junior Child," by Whitley, and "Junior Method in the Church School," by Powell. The teacher who is not willing to pay the price required for such preparation is lacking in that kind of realization of the importance of the task of leading young souls in the way of life that is essential to real success.

But the teacher must also know her pupils individually, their personal traits, their home life, their special aptitudes and interests. The timid or reticent child cannot be dealt with in the same way as the forward or self-assertive child, nor the backward child in the same way as the unusually intelligent child. And every child, whatever may be his disposition or natural capacities, must be approached through some existing interest. The junior worker, therefore, must seek to discover what is already in the child's mind and what he really cares for, and then she must be able to convince him that what is of interest to him is of interest to her also.

A young man found it difficult to maintain order in a class of junior boys whom he was teaching in the Sunday school and to command their attention. After studying the situation carefully, he discovered that there was one lad who was evidently the leader of the group, and he determined to make a friend of this particular boy. Having learned that the boy delivered the evening paper on the street on which he lived, the teacher watched for an opportunity to engage him in conversation as he passed by on his afternoon round. The opportunity soon came, and then other opportunities, until within a short while the teacher had learned a good deal about the boy's life. He was the captain of a football team, and the teacher immediately became interested in this team and its doings. He inquired about its membership, its equipment, and where and when the games were played. By and by he was invited to attend some of these games and to act as umpire, and of course these invitations were enthusiastically accepted. So step by step he won his way to the heart of the young leader and his group, and, because he was interested in what concerned them, they became interested in what concerned him. From being the problem of the teacher the boy leader became his staunch friend and supporter. As a result confusion and inattention were soon changed into order and interest, and it was not long until all the members of the class declared their allegiance to Christ and were received into the Church.

This incident illustrates several of the conditions of success in dealing with juniors. The teacher succeeded in winning the personal admiration and confidence of his pupils and by so doing awakened their interest in the message which he sought to convey to them and in the Saviour whom he sought to reveal to them. And then, by engaging them in activities which were the normal expression of the impressions made by his teaching, he deepened and fixed these impressions until they became dominating influences in their lives

II. THE CENTRAL AIM AND HOW TO ACCOMPLISH IT

The whole effort of the junior worker should be to awaken the religious interest of her pupils, to develop in them an appreciation of Christian ideals, to encourage them in the cultivation of proper attitudes, and to center the whole life of each child about the personality of Christ. That is, her entire task is an evangelistic task. This does not mean that an attempt should be made to give each lesson a specifically evangelistic application. It does mean, however, that, whatever course of lessons she may chance to be using, her constant aim

109

should be to develop in each child love and reverence for Christ, a vital faith in Christ, a growing understanding of what loyalty to Christ demands, and an ever-increasing desire and ability to meet its demands.

1. She should constantly pray and confidently expect that, as a result of this process, the pupils will be brought into a vital personal relation with Christ, and she should watch for signs of growing interest in them and for the opportune moment to approach them with definite appeals for open declaration of their allegiance. In some instances it may be best to wait until the influence of her teaching is recruited through the special season of evangelism appointed for the whole school. The teacher, however, should be on her guard against falling into the habit of waiting for such special seasons. The opportune moment is the moment when real vital interest has been awakened; and, if she is really faithful in her work, that may come at any time. The utmost care should be taken to see that when the appeal is presented the circumstances are as favorable as they can possibly be made. A quiet room and an atmosphere of reverence are absolutely essential; and, if such conditions cannot be secured in the school on Sunday, the teacher should provide for a meeting at some hour during the week.

Whether the appeal to pupils should be made in private, personal interviews, or to the class as a whole depends upon circumstances. If there is a natural leader in the class, it may be best to approach him privately if favorable conditions for doing so can be brought about. For instance, a quiet walk in the coun-

110

try, in which subjects of common interest and pleasant conversation may be found in birds and animals and trees and flowers, may readily become a fitting occasion for drawing the child's attention to the Creator to whom we are indebted for all of our blessings and for leading up to conversation about the duty of giving our lives in loving obedience to him. In case the teacher succeeds in her endeavor, the way will be open for an affective approach to the entire class the following Sunday. There will be other cases, however, in which the teacher will be so sure of her ground that she may with confidence venture upon making her first appeal to the class as a whole. In all cases it should be made in a simple and unconventional way, as if it were taken for granted that to become a follower of Christ was the perfectly natural and proper thing for every right-thinking boy and girl.

Their acknowledgment of Jesus as the Lord of their lives having been made and their allegiance to him openly declared, the teacher should feel free to engage her pupils in friendly conversation about the meaning of the Christian life. The conversation, however, should be directed mainly toward the positive and concrete aspects of this life. They must clearly understand that there are many things which a Christian cannot do, but care should be taken to interpret religion to them in terms of privilege and opportunity rather than in terms of prohibition. And it should be kept constantly in mind that they are interested in the outward expression of religion rather than in the analysis of inward experiences. Of course they have such

111

experiences, but they do not put them under the microscope for the purpose of minutely studying them. In other words, they are not given to introspection and self-examination, and hence are apt either to become mere actors and imitators or to fall into embarrassment and confusion when we attempt to get them to talk about their religious experiences.

2. I have spoken of the fact that junior boys and girls may need to be converted as well as regenerated. That is, they may have definitely entered upon the wrong road, so that it may be necessary for them to face about and start in another direction. It should be observed, however, that children of this age, however unfortunate they may have been in their previous training, are never sinners in the same sense in which an adult may be a sinner. They have not definitely chosen the life of wrongdoing and rebellion against God, but have simply yielded to wayward impulses. There are a number of words in the Bible that are translated by our English word "sin." One of these means simply "missing the mark." Children are sinners in the sense which this word implies; they have made no definite choice of evil, but have simply yielded to outward appeals to their lower natures.

Experiences of deep penitence and of sudden conversion are, therefore, to be expected of them only in exceptional cases. A junior child may be acutely penitent for a definite act of sin, but such a sense of being a sinner as is often felt by adolescents as well as by adults is an unusual experience for children of this age. In fact, as has already been noted, their thoughts are occupied almost entirely with concrete objects and situations and their understanding of such abstract terms as "sin" and "salvation" is exceedingly limited. The junior's decision for Christ may, therefore, as a rule, be expected to come as the quiet culmination of a progressively developing process of spiritual awakening.

3. After the junior has been brought to a definite surrender to Christ, his attention should be called to the reasons for uniting with the Church. For the junior age is the opportune time for taking this important step, since, while the junior is still in some sense an individualist, the group spirit has already begun to develop in him. Practically all boys and girls of this age are members of gangs and clubs of one kind or another, and loyalty to the groups to which they belong is one of their striking characteristics. I read recently a letter from a ten-year-old girl that was taken up almost entirely with an account of a kind of informal club to which she belonged. The members had devised a lot of club secrets, had discovered a private meeting place which was supposed to be unknown to their elders, and had mapped out an extensive course of nature studies. In other words, junior boys and girls are in process of becoming socialized and of learning how to live with others. And especially do they desire to be associated with others in doing things in which they are interested.

It is entirely possible, therefore, to present the Church to them in a way that will make a strong appeal to them. In the Indiana Survey referred to in a previous chapter 6,194 names from forty-three States were secured with verified dates of birth and accession to the

Church. And it is a significant fact that the curve of accession for the 2,234 Methodists included in this list reaches its highest point in the last junior year. This means that under proper conditions we may expect a very large proportion of our junior boys and girls to unite with the Church, and it is quite certain that this expectation is actually realized in many of our best schools. A junior superintendent who had been in service for a number of years wrote me some time ago that practically all of her pupils had been received into the Church before being promoted to the Intermediate Department.

In the instruction designed to awaken in juniors a desire to become members of the Church the negative demands of Church membership will require a certain amount of attention. They should not, however, be put in the forefront. That is, they should not be so presented as to make the children feel that the chief function of the Church is to hedge about their lives with all sorts of prohibitions. On the contrary, the Church should be presented to them as a challenge to coöperation in a great and glorious task, a task a thousand times bigger and finer than that of the Chamber of Commerce, the Farmers' or Merchants' Exchange, and all the clubs and lodges they ever heard about. To this end the teacher should make a brief survey of the various kinds of service which the Church in the name of Christ is seeking to render humanity, and should show her pupils that joining the Church means that they are to have a part in the big task of relieving distress and suffering, abolishing injustice and wrongdoing, and bringing the whole world into one great brotherhood under the leadership of Jèsus Christ.

Through such a course the child may not only be led to desire membership in the Church, but may be definitely prepared for it. Of course it will be necessary before the act of formal acceptance to explain the vows that are to be taken and carefully and intelligently to provide for making the occasion as beautiful and impressive as possible. This, however, will be considered in a subsequent lesson.

III. THE JUNIOR CHILD IN THE CHURCH

The child in the Church is still but a babe in Christ, and it will require years of patient teaching and training to bring him to the fullness of Christian manhood.

1. His religion is rather a matter of personal loyalty than of vital intellectual conviction. His understanding of Christian doctrines and of the larger practical and social implications of Christian discipleship is exceedingly limited. These, therefore, must be gradually unfolded to him as his intellectual and spiritual capacities develop. Like the Boy of Nazareth, as he increases in stature he must increase also in wisdom, and it is the business of the Sunday school to furnish the conditions of such healthy and normal growth.

2. The junior child's will is still unstable and his emotions ephemeral; while at the same time, as has already been noted, he is fairly bubbling over with physical energy. We should not be surprised, therefore, to find in his life what appear to us gross inconsistencies. The teacher, for instance, need not be disappointed if

115

the boys in her class who have expressed their purpose to be followers of Christ and their desire to enter into the fellowship of the Church are discovered a few minutes later pulling each other's hair or shooting paper balls across the room or if they are found the next day engaged in a hot dispute on the playground. Such manifestations should not be regarded as indications of lack of sincerity, but rather as expressions of the abounding energy of b ings who have but limited powers of moral discrimination and have not yet acquired those habits of self-control which may come in later years. The cultivation of such habits should be one of the teacher's aims, and along with it should go the cultivation of such qualities as chivalry, generosity, helpfulness, and coöperation, and of such attitudes as trust in God, happiness, gratitude, honor, obedience, courage, sympathy, and loyalty. This means that the teacher should not only talk to her pupils about these things, but that she should seek in every possible way to provide opportunities for their expression. This is necessary for two reasons.

In the first place, generalizations are impossible for children of this age. For instance, it is not sufficient to set before them the ideal of honesty, but they must be shown what this ideal requires in all sorts of concrete situations—that it not only means that they must not take what does not belong to them, but also that they must not cheat in examinations nor deceive their parents nor take an unfair advantage of those on the other side in a game of ball or marbles.

In the second place, it is only through continuous

116

practice that right ideals may be established and right attitudes made habitual. The teacher, therefore, should take pains to call the attention of her pupils to opportunities that come up in the class and to such opportunities as are likely to come up in their everyday social relations, in the home, in the school, on the playgrounds, for putting into practice the virtues that are illustrated in the life of Jesus and in the lives of many of his followers. She should also be on the lookout for opportunities to engage them in such special activities as will serve as normal channels for the expression of the types of interest that are awakened within them through vital contact with Jesus. Many such opportunities may be found in connection with the local Church and community. Others may be found in the larger activities and enterprises of the denomination as a whole, especially in the field of missions. Valuable help in discovering such opportunities may be obtained through community surveys, through literature prepared by the various denominational boards, and by the reading of such books as "The Project Principle in Religious Education," by Shaver, and "One Hundred Projects for the Church School," by Towner.

3. Officers and teachers should unite in a common aim to generate in the Sunday school an atmosphere of friendliness and reverence. Such an atmosphere is as essential to the spiritual development of the child as fresh air and sunshine are to his physical development. And it is difficult to create such an atmosphere in a single class unless it pervades the entire school. This means that it must be the product of a group spirit,

that all the official staff of the school must themselves be earnestly and vitally religious, and that their bearing toward one another and toward the pupils must be such as to make clear the fact that Christ is the center of the friendly circle and that all hearts turn to him with love and adoration.

SUGGESTIONS FOR STUDY

1. What two general groups of juniors are mentioned in this chapter?

2. What difficulties in approaching Group Two are mentioned? Can you think of others?

3. What requisites for dealing successfully with children of this group are mentioned? What others would you suggest?

4. Mention some of the ways which the junior worker may employ in gaining adequate understanding of her pupils. What plan have you found most effective?

5. What plans have you found most effective in appealing to juniors to decide to be Christians?

6. What type of conversion experience may normally be expected of juniors?

7. What is the best way of presenting to juniors the matter of joining the Church?

8. What should be expected of juniors and what methods of dealing with them should be employed after they have become members of the Church?

118

CHAPTER VIII

EARLY AND MIDDLE ADOLESCENCE

I. THE DAWN OF ADOLESCENCE

SOMETIME between the beginning of the twelfth and the end of the thirteenth year the child enters upon the most momentous change that ever comes to a human life. For it is during this period that those physical functions which are related to the perpetuation of the race begin to awaken, and with their awakening the unfolding life is overwhelmed with a veritable flood of new emotions and interests and problems. It is the beginning of full selfhood, the completion of the cycle of physical and psychical powers which constitute one a separate, self-directing, and responsible individual. But while it marks a new stage in the development of self-consciousness, it marks also a new stage in the development of social consciousness. As the youth comes to realize in a new way his separate individuality and his right to live out his own life, he comes also to a new realization of his relation to others, and fellowship, life-sharing, and social responsibility take on wider and deeper meanings. He begins to ask why, not in the light and careless fashion of early childhood, but with a grim earnestness that will not allow him to rest until some satisfactory answer is discovered. Abstractions and generalizations begin to interest him. He becomes an idealist. He dreams dreams and builds castles in the air. He is enamored of perfection, haunted by

119

visions of truth and beauty and triumphant manhood, and cannot be persuaded that they are beyond the possibility of realization. And naturally and inevitably his soul is swept by all sorts of conflicting emotions. Faith and doubt, hope and despair, exhilaration and depression, arrogant self-confidence and painful self-depreciation contend for the mastery of his soul. He is confused, perplexed, tossed to and fro by contradictory impulses, the meaning of which he does not understand. But whatever clouds and mists may gather above him and about him, the gleam still shines before him and beckons him onward and upward.

The essential quality of his ideals and visions will necessarily be largely determined by his previous associations and training. These may have been such as to have led him to the conclusion that the supreme achievement in life would be to become an elegant loafer or a successful crook or a noted desperado. In other words, his estimate as to what is really admirable and worth while may be utterly and totally erroneous. But, however sadly he may have been misled by his former teachers and guides, he is still, according to the light that he possesses, an dealist bent on making his dreams come true. I once heard ex-Senator W. R. Webb, who has been for more than half a century at the head of the most famous training school for boys in the South, say that, among all the thousands of boys with whom he had been brought into intimate contact, he had never known one who meant to be a good-for-nothing. Many of them, because of wrong or inadequate training, had very erroneous conceptions as to what the real meaning and the true values of life are, but every one of them intended to achieve success as he understood it.

II. A CRITICAL PERIOD

We should naturally expect that such a crisis would be found upon investigation to mark an exceedingly critical and important epoch in the developing life, and this expectation is justified both by the collective experience of mankind and by modern scientific research.

1. Take, for instance, the profoundly significant fact that for untold ages half-savage tribes, as well as great civilized peoples, have followed the custom of initiating their youth into the mysteries of their religion soon after the dawn of adolescence. A Jewish boy, we remember, became "a son of the law" at the age of twelve, and Christian Churches that practice confirmation administer this rite to those brought up under their instruction at about the same age.

2. Recent investigations in regard to this period have brought out the following facts:

(1) It is an age of excessive criminality. A large proportion of those who are convicted as lawbreakers begin their criminal careers before the close of middle adolescence.

(2) It is the age in which the greatest losses occur to the Sunday school. Researches carried on in many widely separated localities show that a fearfully large percentage of those who have been regular attendants at Sunday school during early and later childhood

121

drop out between twelve and sixteen. The Indiana Survey, previously referred to, revealed the fact that in the urban schools investigated the tendency to break away began in the thirteenth year, that in the rural schools it began in the twelfth year, and that in both types the elimination in the case of boys proceeded so rapidly that more than two-thirds of those who were members of Sunday schools at twelve dropped out before reaching the age of seventeen. While the percentages for girls differed considerably from those for boys, they showed the same tendency to a steady decline during the period of early and middle adolescence.

(3) It is the period in which a larger number of people unite with the Church than in any other. Of the 6,194 cases investigated in the Indiana Survey, about 41 per cent became members of the Church between twelve and seventeen. This is probably not far from the average for the Church as a whole; and if so, about thirty per cent more persons become Church members during these six years than in all the years that follow.

III. SOME ADOLESCENT CHARACTERISTICS

It is evident from these facts that the intermediate-senior age is a period of peculiar danger and that it is also a period of special opportunity for those who are interested in the evangelistic work of the Church in the building of the kingdom of God. All this may be made clearer by a somewhat more careful study of certain of the adolescent characteristics mentioned above.

1. The awakening of the sense of selfhood leads naturally to a tendency to self-assertion and rebellion

against all sorts of external restraints. Boys and girls who, up to this time, have been reasonably docile and obedient often become stubborn and self-willed and resentful of authority. Of course such an attitude is fraught with serious peril and may lead to disastrous consequences. And yet, when we come to study the causes which lie back of it, it becomes at once apparent that, instead of being taken as a sign of innate mean-ness, as is too often the case, it should be regarded as a necessary stage in the development of individual life. The necessity for cheerful obedience to rightful au-thority is one of the lessons which every one must learn in order to attain a complete and useful life, and this lesson we must manage to bring home to our boys and girls. But self-confidence, individuality, and personal initiative are also essential to successful living. We do not want our youth to become mere imitators and fol-lowers. We want them to learn to think for themselves, to face courageously their own problems and responsi-bilities, and to become creators and leaders. The method of dealing with them, therefore, should not be that of repression, but of sympathetic guidance. They have now reached the age of reason, and we should seek so to win their respect and confidence that we may be able to show them to what end we are seeking to direct them and why certain kinds of discipline and self-restraint are necessary to the attainment of these ends. Many parents and teachers fail sadly at this point. Instead of respecting the individuality of the teen-age boys and girls for whose destiny they are in a measure responsible and patiently and tactfully seeking to lead them toward the goal which they desire that they shall attain, they undertake by all sorts of compulsion to force them to act as they think young people ought to act. The result may be disastrous in either one or two directions. In the case of the pliant and yielding youth it may effectually destroy all independence and power of initiative and make of him a permanent weakling. In the case of the vigorous and aggressive youth it may lead to defiance and rebellion. Almost any intelligent observer can call to mind illustrations of both of these types.

2. Again, it is almost inevitable that the first attempts of the youth to discover the reasons that lie back of the things which he has been taught to believe and to do should lead in most cases to bewildered and painful perplexity and in some cases to harassing and paralyzing doubt.

(1) Doctor James Bissett Pratt thinks that a great deal of so-called adolescent doubt is entirely superficial. Teen-age boys and girls, he maintains, learn from their teachers and from the books they read that they are passing through an age of doubt and hear their associates talking glibly about their intellectual difficulties. So they decide that doubt for them is the natural and proper thing and that in this, as in other matters of common social convention, they must conform to type. There is probably a good deal of truth in this contention. For it is a mistake to assume that the average youth—or the average adult either, for that matter—finds himself under any intellectual compulsion to rationalize either his religion or any other fundamen-

124

tal experience of his life. As a matter of fact, the average person, either young or old, is very much inclined to accept the customs and beliefs and standards and ideals that are handed down to him, or that are current in the circle in which he moves, without raising any serious questions about them. And this is particularly true of religious beliefs, which are generally associated with the unquestionable reality and satisfaction of religious experience.

(2) There is always a considerable minority, however, who find themselves driven by an inner necessity to ask why they should believe certain things and adhere to certain practices and reject others. The writer was brought up in a Christian home and in a simple, rural community in which practically everybody believed implicitly in the Bible as God's revelation to man. So far as he now recalls, he never in his childhood heard its authority challenged. And yet sometime between the age of twelve and the age of fourteen he found himself involved in a maze of terrifying uncertainty as to everything that he had been taught. How he was temporarily delivered from the perplexity into which he had fallen need not be considered here, the point of emphasis being simply the fact that these doubts arose without any suggestion from the outside. That many earnest and sincerely religious boys and girls pass through a similar experience is beyond question.

As the thoughtful youth advances from early to middle and later adolescence his doubts often take on a different complexion and become still more serious and bewildering. For then he begins to face problems that are much less easy of solution than those by which he was confronted in the earlier period, problems growing out of his relation to a living world in which everything is in a state of perpetual change. If we were in a static world, it would be comparatively easy for each generation to hand down to the succeeding generation a definite set of opinions expressed in terms that need never be changed and that would need only to be memorized and comprehended by the young of each new age. But the situation is very different in a world whose most striking characteristics are unceasing flux and movement. Men are forever discovering new facts or larger meanings in and applications of facts already known, and, as a result, our institutions, our industrial organizations and methods, our social customs and relations, our world outlook, and even the very language through which we express our thoughts and emotions are constantly changing. Such changes necessarily require all sorts of intellectual readjustments. Truth abides unchanged through all ages. Christ remains the same yesterday, to-day, and forever. But each generation must interpret both in terms of its own life experiences and must find out for itself how its new discoveries are to be fitted into and made to harmonize with its inherited beliefs. And the fact that the earnest and intelligent youth of each age must face this big and bewilderingly difficult task must never be lost sight of by those who seek to guide them in the way of life and establish them in their religious faith.

(3) Account should also be taken of the fact that adolescent doubts, even when they are the result of sugges-

tion of one kind or another, are often quite real and need to be dealt with intelligently and tactfully. Indeed, the very fact that doubters of this kind are much less serious in their quest for truth than are those described in the preceding paragraphs often makes it all the more difficult to handle them successfully.

(4) Specific suggestions as to methods of dealing with these various types of doubt will be taken up in the next chapter, the thing upon which I wish to insist here being the importance of dealing with all of them intelligently and sympathetically. This means, for one thing, that, instead of lumping them together and branding them as heinous sins, we are to seek to understand each individual case and to treat it in the way that promises to bring about the surest and speediest cure. For, while there are without question cases in which youthful doubt is in part an apology for willful disregard of recognized ideals, such cases are probably exceptional. In most instances it is brought about in one of the ways mentioned above. That is, it is the result of the sincere efforts of immature minds either to translate the naïve, unquestioning faith of childhood into the rational and stable faith of dawning manhood and womanhood or to harmonize their inherited beliefs with a lot of new knowledge that has come into their possession.

The impulse that prompts such efforts is entirely laudable, however crude and awkward may be these initial endeavors. The baby would never learn to walk who never tried to walk. Instead, therefore, of attempting to carry him forever in our arms, we encourage him to try his own feeble and tottering legs even at the risk of getting a few falls and bumps. Meanwhile, however, we keep close by his side and lend him such help as may be required in order to make sure that no serious harm shall befall him. And if he stumbles a bit, we do not scold him, but encourage him to try again.

Just so we should treat our older boys and girls who are trying to get a firmer and a more intelligent grasp of "the faith which was once for all delivered unto the saints." Often the most disastrous thing we can do is to make them feel that, because they are perplexed, they are condemned sinners. Many have been driven in this way into permanent skepticism. What they need is not repression and rebuke, but encouragement and guidance. We should seek to help them to understand that their doubts are not the results of their superior wisdom and mental ability, but are simply such difficulties as frequently arise when young people whose experience and information are exceedingly limited first undertake seriously to grapple with the great problems of life. At the same time we should teach them that, instead of tamely yielding to their doubts, they should, like the hero of Tennyson's "In Memoriam," resolutely fight the specters of the mind and conquer them—in other words, that it is not only their right but their imperative duty to *will* to believe the things that make for their salvation and for the salvation of the world. For the rest, it is our business to supply them with such rational motives and to bring them under the power of such gracious influences, human and divine, as will enable them to achieve the victory which we desire for them.

128

3. Another characteristic of youth to which attention has been called is its idealism. Because the eager expectation that kindles in the heart of the adolescent is but slightly restrained as yet by those habits of caution which develop in later life, he is inclined to all sorts of reckless and daring experiments. He is impatient of delay. He is inclined to regard prudence as a species of timidity which merits only contempt. Better the desperate and fatal "Charge of the Light Brigade," he is apt to think, than waiting behind bulwarks for a more favorable occasion.

As a consequence of this tendency to rash and heedless adventure many gallant barks that set sail in the morning with confidence and enthusiasm soon go to wreck on the breakers. The world is full of these wrecks, pathetic witnesses of high hopes shattered and high ambitions which ended in tragedy.

And yet what an opportunity this same characteristic of youth offers to the Church! For where else can we find an ideal that would bear one moment's comparison in its appeal to the dreaming, aspiring, longing souls of our boys and girls with the ideal of Jesus? And what other task so thrilling in its challenge as that of becoming Christ's fellow worker in building on the earth a triumphant kingdom of God?

Here again our work, as teaching evangelists, is to see that a fine, normal impulse, instead of being allowed to go astray, is directed to proper ends and guided into proper channels.

4. One more characteristic of youth that may be mentioned is the awakening of the social nature. The

adolescent spells friendship with a capital "F." He longs for companionship and readily forms deep and ardent attachments. This makes him peculiarly susceptible to social influences; and if these influences chance to be bad, they easily lead him astray. Herein lies one of the greatest perils of youth. But herein also lies what is perhaps the supreme opportunity of the Church in its relation to adolescents. For, if they are responsive to unworthy friendships, they are also responsive to those that are ennobling. They are still hero worshipers; and, while they may easily be led through the manifestation of certain striking personal qualities to admire and follow men of ignoble character, they are quite as ready to yield their allegiance to the noble and worthy, provided they are approached in the right way. This at once suggests a number of considerations that are exceedingly important for those who are seeking to lead boys and girls of this age into the Christian life. It will be sufficient barely to enumerate these considerations here.

(1) The first to be mentioned is the importance of the teacher's own personality and the necessity of approaching his pupil through vital and intimate personal friendship.

(2) The next is the possibility of utilizing the friendly atmosphere of the Church, the Sunday school, and the class as effective evangelistic agencies.

(3) Most significant of all, however, is the fact that Christ, if he be adequately revealed, exactly satisfies the dominant longing of the heart of youth. For the quest of the adolescent is for the ideal of heroism, and

nowhere else is this ideal fully personified except in Jesus Christ. The youth yearns, not for friendship only, but for ideal friendship; and, in spite of all the sneering skepticism of the world, he continues steadfastly to believe in it. The blossoming period of this high faith and aspiration is a peculiarly opportune time for revealing to him Jesus Christ as the supreme and all-sufficient Friend, the Friend in whose love and companionship all his dreams may be realized.

SUGGESTIONS FOR STUDY

1. Discuss in general terms the meaning of adolescence.

2. Consider all the facts you can recall tending to show that this is a period (a) of unusual danger and (b) of unusual opportunity.

3. Discuss briefly the four characteristics of adolescence specially considered in this chapter.

4. Discuss the differences between early and middle adolescence.

5. Discuss the following question: What significance have the facts here presented for the teacher of religion?

CHAPTER IX

EARLY AND MIDDLE ADOLESCENCE
(CONTINUED)

THE previous chapter was devoted to a study of some of the important characteristics of early and middle adolescence. With this study as a background, we may now proceed to a consideration of some of the practical methods of dealing with boys and girls of this age.

I. GENERAL ADAPTATION OF EVANGELISTIC AGENCIES

Let us in the beginning remind ourselves once more of what we are seeking to accomplish. Our aim is to bring these boys and girls to a living, personal faith in Christ as their Lord and Saviour and to help them toward an increasing appreciation of the ideals of Christ and an increasing understanding and practice of the teachings of Christ.

Before beginning this study the reader should carefully review what is said in Chapter III about evangelistic agencies, meanwhile keeping in mind the fact that, while all of these agencies are to be used in the evangelization of adolescents, careful attention must be given to the adaptation of each to the requirements of adolescent life.

1. The fact that boys and girls of this age are peculiarly responsive to the appeal of friendship gives the teacher or pastor a unique opportunity of reaching

132

them through his personal influence. It is generally agreed by those who have made a careful study of this period from the religious viewpoint that nothing else counts for so much in the educational process as the character of the teacher made effective through real vital friendship. It is often assumed that a great gulf is fixed between the adolescent and the adult over which neither can pass, that neither can understand the other, and that therefore intimate friendship between them is impossible. That there are difficulties in the way of mutual understanding is beyond question. Many parents lose their hold on their children, many teachers on their pupils, because of inability on each side to understand the other. I do not believe, however, that such a condition is necessary. On the contrary, I believe that the gulf between youth and adulthood may be bridged and that the twain may meet in mutual appreciation and friendship. The initiative, however, must be made by the parent or pastor or teacher. He has already passed through the varied experiences of youth and ought, therefore, to be able, by refreshing his memory through reading and personal association and observation, to approach those who are still in the midst of these experiences. To the youth, on the other hand, the experiences of the adult are a *terra incognita*, and it is only step by step that he can come to a real understanding of the viewpoint of his elders. But he will readily come to a kind of intuitive appreciation of the fact that his father or his mother or his teacher understands him and is in vital sympathy with him,

133

and this furnishes sufficient ground for a real friendship between them.

(1) Friendship with youth must be on a basis somewhat different from friendship with the younger child. It must be real comradeship and not the gracious condescension of a superior to an inferior. The teacher of adolescents who cannot be a real companion of his pupils, sharing all their normal interests, cannot become an effective leader.

(2) The successful leader of youth must be the kind of person whom healthy-minded boys and girls admire. All young people are enamored of physical strength and prowess. It would be well, therefore, if every teacher of adolescents could be an Apollo Belvedere or a Juno Sospita. This, however, is by no means essential; for experience proves that intelligence, pluck, and force of character may more than make up for lack of physical vigor. No youth would think of withholding his admiration from the hero of Trafalgar because he was a physical weakling. We knew a young pastor who became the hero of a group of adolescent boys and girls notwithstanding the fact that he was a cripple and small of stature. For, in spite of his physical limitations, he not only planned and directed their sports, but actually took part in them. Those who have made a study of boys' clubs and gangs tell us that the leaders of these groups are often chosen solely on the basis of their mental and moral qualifications and that in many cases those selected are by no means conspicuous in the matter of physical strength.

(3) Since the fundamental aim of the teacher is to

lead his pupils to a living faith in Christ, he must not only be thoroughly loyal to Christ, but must in some measure illustrate the Christ ideal in his own life. The mingled strength and beauty of this ideal can in no other way be so effectively revealed as through personal character.

2. As regards the content of instruction the principle of adaptation requires that those aspects of our Lord's life and teachings which answer to the intellectual and spiritual needs of youth shall be placed in the forefront.

(1) They are dreaming of ideal manhood and at the same time are inclined to interpret the ideal in terms of heroic daring and achievement. Show them Christ as the ideal Man and the ideal Hero, "the purest among the mighty and the mightiest among the pure, who with his pierced hands lifted empires off their hinges and turned the course of history into new channels," but who also was tender to the poor and lowly and loved little children and took them up in his arms and blessed them.

(2) They long for friendship, vital, intimate, satisfying. Reveal Christ to them as the one all-sufficient Friend, the Friend who is always near, always understands, never betrays nor disappoints. And show then how through trust and self-surrender they may come into a vital personal relation with him.

(3) In many cases boys and girls of this age are painfully conscious of a wide discrepancy between the ideals they cherish and their actual achievements in conduct. Often they are overwhelmed with a sense of sin and of their utter helplessness in the face of the

135

temptations that beset them. Those who have a vivid recollection of their own youth will readily understand me when I say that there is no class of human beings who suffer more poignantly as a result of their recognized limitations and shortcomings than adolescents. Christ should be revealed to them, therefore, not only as a Friend who understands them, pities them, loves them with an everlasting love, but also as a Saviour who is willing and able to deliver them and keep them. Illustrations of what he may do for those who trust him and long to be like him and to serve and triumph as he served and triumphed may be drawn from the Bible, from the history of the Church, and from personal observation.

(4) Adolescents want to engage in great enterprises involving adventure, daring, and self-sacrifice; and an enterprise is all the more challenging in its appeal to them if it involves helping others. Knight-errantry was a product of the youth of our modern world, and the spirit of which it was the expression is reproduced in the heart of each generation of boys and girls. We should seek, therefore, to show them that the call of Christ is a call to service, to self-sacrifice, to high and heroic daring, and that he who enlists under the banner of Christ enlists in the biggest and the most important undertaking that was ever launched on the earth. And, because of their widening social interest, this is the opportune time to begin to explain to them more fully and definitely than is possible in the case of junior children what this undertaking involves, that it means working with God for the banishment of injustice and

ignorance and greed and selfishness in all its hideous forms and for bringing the world into one great brotherhood of peace and good will under the leadership of Jesus Christ. There are not many normal youths who will not respond with eager enthusiasm to the appeal of such a program if it is presented to them in terms that they can understand.

3. As to the method of instruction, the principle of adaptation requires that the personality and ideals of Christ shall be presented concretely rather than as a series of abstract propositions. That is, they should be presented in the form of vivid word pictures, portraying and interpreting incidents in the life of Christ and stories drawn from Church history illustrating the meaning of these incidents.

Objection has often been made to the use of what is known as extra-Biblical material in religious education. Those who raise such objection, however, overlook the fact that one of the most effective ways of making the Christian message clear and vital to the child or youth is through biographical pictures showing how the principles taught by Christ work out in human life.

> "For Wisdom dealt with mortal powers,
>   Where truth in closest words shall fail,
>   When truth embodied in a tale
> Shall enter in at lowly doors."

But the biographical story drawn from Church history has another value besides that of illustrating the meaning of the Christian life. It serves to impress upon the mind of youth the fact that the Christ whom they

137

are called upon to revere and love and follow is not a dead hero-saint, but a living, ever-present Friend and Saviour, who through these nineteen hundred years has been literally fulfilling his promise made to his disciples before his ascension, "Lo, I am with you alway, even unto the end of the world." The agency most relied upon by the ancient Hebrews in the religious education of their children was the stories of the great providential events in their national life and of the deeds of their national heroes. It was thus that they brought home to each new generation a sense of Jehovah's presence and care and a realization of his power and holiness.

For these reasons I am persuaded that in our evangelistic work with adolescents large use should be made of biographical material drawn from the annals of the Christian Church as well as from the Bible. The use of such material is rendered all the more feasible by the fact that, if the stories of heroic lives and religiously significant events are properly presented, boys and girls of this age will read them with deep and intense interest.

4. There must be adaptation also in the matter of atmosphere and worship.

(1) Boys and girls of this age are peculiarly responsive to an atmosphere of friendliness, brotherhood, and cheerful comradeship, and everything possible should be done in order to create such an atmosphere in the Church and in the Sunday school. Many of us will recall the feeling of disappointment that came over us when we first began to suspect that perhaps the Church

was not just the kind of brotherhood we had supposed it to be. Is it not possible that the awakening of such a suspicion marks the beginning, in many cases, of the alienation of our boys and girls from the Church? At any rate, friendliness and mutual care and consideration are fundamental characteristics of a true Christian brotherhood, and our boys and girls have a right to expect that their awakened social natures shall find in the Sunday school and the Church an atmosphere that answers to their social needs.

(2) While adolescents are not apt to be demonstrative, they are, as a rule, deeply emotional and respond readily to all sorts of appeals to worthy sentiment. If properly led, therefore, they will enter heartily into a service of worship, provided the prayers and songs and Scripture readings selected are within the range of their comprehension and answer to the real longings and aspirations of their hearts. Great care should be given, therefore, to planning worship services for pupils of this age. It is, of course, impossible, in the brief space allotted to me here, to give specific directions. Indeed, every one who is responsible for such services should not only study the specific needs of his own particular group, but should endeavor to qualify himself for leading them by seeking such suggestions as may be obtained through the reading of magazine articles and books on worship and by making sure before entering upon the service that he himself is in a thoroughly worshipful spirit. Some of the books that might be profitably used for this purpose are: Hartshorne, "Manual for Training in Worship"; Gibson, "Serv-

139

ices of Worship for Boys"; Weigle and Tweedy, "Training the Devotional Life." It may be remarked in passing, however, that long, desultory talks and rambling prayers should be studiously avoided, that the hymns used should be dignified and should express in true poetic form sentiments that naturally appeal to the heart of youth, and that the program should be arranged with the view of the largest possible participation on the part of the pupils.

5. Intermediate and senior boys and girls will engage enthusiastically in promoting the social, educational, charitable, and missionary work of the Church, provided the nature and meaning of such work is concretely and clearly set before them and provided such tasks are offered as appeal to their normal interests. In most cases it will be best to present to them a variety of types of service and allow them to choose, under proper guidance, the particular types they will undertake. Some of these should always be immediately connected with the work of the Church in the local community and should be such as involve immediate contacts with persons to whom service is to be rendered. For suggestions in regard to work for adolescents the teacher is referred to "The Project Principle in Religious Education," Part II, Sections Four, Five, and Six, by Shaver, and to "One Hundred Projects for the Church School," by Towner. Every teacher of intermediates and seniors should also keep in constant touch with the Department of Missionary Education of our General Sunday School Board.

140

II. INDIVIDUAL ADAPTATION

In any intermediate or senior class or department there are likely to be pupils of several quite different types. For instance, there may be some whose early religious education has been partially or totally neglected; some who have already become in a very real and positive sense sinners; some who, while fully purposing in their hearts to be loyal to Christ, have for one cause or another fallen into doubt or into uncertainty about their religious experiences; and some who, having been brought up in the nurture and admonition of the Lord, have passed from childhood to adolescence without any marked religious crisis. And, besides the variations growing out of differences of individuality, there will be others occasioned by the stages of development which the pupils have reached. For while, for lack of space, I have been compelled to consider early and middle adolescents as one group, there are in reality striking differences between the boy or girl of thirteen and the boy or girl of seventeen, and it is essential that these differences shall be taken account of by one who would become a successful teacher of youth. That is, the teacher must not only seek to acquaint himself with the home life, the previous training and habits, and the personal peculiarities of each pupil, but must consider all of them in relation to the pupil's age and physical and mental development.

1. If the teacher is to deal wisely with pupils of these several types, he must study them individually. To this end, he must visit their homes in order that he may

get a first-hand acquaintance with the conditions and influences under which they have been brought up and that he may secure the approval and, if possible, the sympathetic coöperation of their parents. And he must seek so to win the confidence of his pupils and to come into such a relation of personal intimacy with them that each of them will be willing to talk to him with perfect freedom about everything that is of interest to him. In this way he ought to be able to acquire such a thorough knowledge of the viewpoint, ideals, interests, moral status, and individual peculiarities of each member of his class as will enable him to discover the best approach to each. And upon the basis of information thus gathered he must determine just what modifications of his methods are to be made in the case of any particular pupil. No definite instruction upon this point can be given because of the vast variety in types and situations. Success here will depend entirely upon the tact and spirit and sympathetic insight of the teacher. The teacher who knows and loves his pupils and is endowed with a reasonable amount of common sense will be able to discover for himself the easy passages to their hearts.

2. While, however, no teacher of youth can succeed who does not study them individually and seek to adapt his methods to the peculiar needs of each one of them, it still remains true that the suggestions offered in the first section of this chapter in regard to the way in which the teacher is to use the various evangelistic agencies are of quite general application. That is, with such modifications in methods of handling as in-

142

dividual peculiarities may require, the same lesson material, the same programs of worship, and the same kinds of activity may be used with all of the types described in the preceding paragraph.

(1) Suppose, for instance, you are seeking to awaken the religious interest of the neglected youth or to arouse the conscience of the indifferent or sinful youth and bring him to a saving faith in Christ, what other way can you take that is likely to prove so effective as that of revealing to him the spirit and ideals of Christ in your own life, progressively interpreting to him the personality, teachings, and work of Christ through an intelligently adapted process of instruction, and deepening and vitalizing all impressions by means of a wholesome religious atmosphere and wisely directed activities?

The teacher should pray with expectant faith that, as a result of his efforts, every one of his pupils may be led to a surrender of his life to Christ, but the time when and the circumstances under which the appeal for such surrender is to be made should be determined very much as in the case of the junior child considered in Chapter VII.

In some instances it will be best to seek for favorable opportunities for talking over the matter of beginning the Christian life with certain members of the class privately and individually and for endeavoring to bring them one by one to the point of definite decision. There will be other instances in which it may be well to make the appeal before the class as a whole, provided the session is held in a quiet room where the teacher may make sure of a proper atmosphere; and still others

143

in which it may best be made to the entire department or before the entire school above the primary grades. In the last two cases, it may be well to seek the help of the pastor or some one else who thoroughly understands the situation and knows how to approach a group of boys and girls. While the invitation service is in progress the doors of the room should be closed and no interruption of any kind should be allowed.

While the worker with intermediates or seniors should studiously avoid suggesting in any way whatsoever that his pupils are to postpone their definite entrance upon the Christian life to some future time when conditions may be more favorable, he should carefully plan to make the most of special evangelistic seasons in behalf of those whom he has failed to bring to positive decision in the regular course of his class work. First among these in its importance for the special type of work we are considering is the annual campaign of evangelism in the Sunday school to be considered in a subsequent chapter. But it is possible also to make effective use of the revival with boys and girls who have reached the age of middle adolescence. Two things, however, need to be said in this connection:

(a) If the Sunday school is what it ought to be, it will rarely be necessary to wait for the revival to bring the pupils who are under its care to a vital personal friendship with Christ. The fact that it often is necessary means that the Sunday school has partially failed in its evangelistic task.

(b) Revival methods need to be employed with great care in the case of boys and girls of this age. For one of their common characteristics is a tendency to intense emotionalism; and, therefore, since their emotions have not yet been brought under the control of the will and reason, they may be easily led into emotional excesses that are likely to prove injurious to them both physically and morally. In certain types such excesses tend to break down nervous control and to bring about a state of nervous instability, and, in so far as this is the case, they weaken the will and debilitate the moral nature. In other types they often result in bitter disappointment and dangerous reaction. In the introduction to a book written by a prominent pastor a few years ago the author told how he had been brought to the verge of despair and temporarily alienated from the Church as a result of just such an adolescent experience. Instead, therefore, of subjecting intermediates and seniors to the kind of appeals that are often found necessary in the case of adults, it is better to take advantage of the community interest awakened by the revival by providing for them special services in which both the messages and the worship programs are adapted to their needs. And in planning such services it is well to remember that, while the youth may be a sinner in a much more real sense than is possible in the case of the older child, he is still not a sinner in the adult sense. For his evil deeds are still much more the results of heedlessness, impulsiveness, lack of judgment and self-control, and inability to resist temptation than of deliberate choice. Furthermore, such sinful habits as he may have formed have not yet become fixed, nor has he reached such a state of moral blindness as befalls the

10   145

transgressor in later life. He is much more open, therefore, to the gracious appeals that come in the manner of the still small voice than is the adult sinner, and hence in his case the methods which must often be employed to awaken the latter and bring him to conviction and repentance are not required.

In Chapter VII attention is called to the fact that no distinct religious crisis is likely to occur in the life of the junior child. It is to be noted here, however, that such crises are quite common in the lives of adolescents. The moment of decision is often distinctly marked and accompanied by deep emotion. Many men and women converted in youth continue throughout their lives to sing with unabated gladness and gratitude,

"O happy day that fixed my choice
On thee, my Saviour and my God!"

Such sharply marked conversion experiences, however, are by no means universal. There are some who come into the new experience of trust and peace very much as the murky skies and the icy deadness of winter are changed to the brightness and warmth of springtime. It all depends on the mental and emotional characteristics of the person involved. The utmost pains should be taken, therefore, to keep the youth from associating regeneration with some special type of emotional experience. We should make clear to him that there is no standard type of conversion experience and that his quest should be for Christ and not for any kind of feeling. In other words, he should be taught that all he need concern himself about is the genuineness of his

146

own surrender to Christ and the sincerity of his purpose to live in loyal allegiance to Christ, leaving the matter of feeling to take care of itself. Peace lies in this direction and increasing joy in fellowship with Christ and in his service. But when the youth begins to set his thoughts on the way he feels, he is almost sure to grow morbid and dissatisfied. Digging into one's feelings is like tearing up a flower in order to test the genuineness of its perfume and its beauty. When the tearing-up process is finished, no flower is left, but only a few broken petals.

(2) When we come to consider the case of adolescents who began the Christian life in childhood and still desire to be loyal in their allegiance to Christ, but who for one cause or another have fallen into doubt and perplexity, we find that the same general principles as to agencies and methods are applicable that are suggested for use with the group considered above, it being still understood that intelligent individual adaptation is always necessary.

There are two general varieties in this group—one composed of those who have become perplexed in their initial efforts to transform the simple inherited beliefs of childhood into the vital convictions of dawning manhood and womanhood; the other composed of those who, finding the religious experiences of childhood no longer adequate, are inclined to doubt whether or not these experiences really possessed any elements of genuineness.

(a) There are certain respects in which both of these cases require special treatment.

147

For instance, a youth belonging to the first group, especially in the period of early adolescence, as was suggested in Chapter VIII, may often be helped by being reminded that his difficulties are partly the result of the fact that his experience and intellectual equipment are not yet sufficient to enable him to grapple successfully with the big questions which his newly awakened sense of selfhood has thrust upon him and that the wise course, therefore, is to hold some of these questions in abeyance until he has had time to acquire a wider experience and a larger fund of information. This does not mean, however, that his difficulties are to be treated lightly or that no effort is to be made to answer his questions. On the contrary, the teacher should in the spirit of sympathetic friendship place himself side by side with his pupils and, frankly recognizing the reality of their problems and the legitimacy of their quest for truth, should do his best to help them to solve these problems and to find the light after which they are groping. This is particularly necessary as the pupils advance into middle and later adolescence. For, as has already been pointed out, the problems that begin to confront them at this stage become both larger and more complex, since, in the case of the more thoughtful and intelligent among them, they involve the necessity of fusing their inherited beliefs and a varied assortment of new facts and experiences that are being thrust upon them into a unified and consistent whole. And while it is still necessary to advise against hasty conclusions and to insist upon the time element as an essential factor in the process of reaching satisfactory solutions, it is also necessary that we shall be able to lead them step by step into a clearer understanding of the reasons why, in spite of all the mystery that surrounds us and all the unanswerable questions that thrust themselves upon us, we still find in the holy Scriptures, in the Word made flesh, and in the verities of Christian experience a sure foundation for a stable and increasingly triumphant faith.

In the case of one belonging to the second group, it is well to explain that the fact that the religion of his childhood carried with it no profound depth of conviction does not mean that it was not real; that the child must necessarily think and feel as a child, but that God may be as truly in his life as in the life of an older person who knows much more and can reason much better. And he ought to be encouraged not to despise his earlier religious experience, but to seek by prayer and obedience to deepen and enrich it.

(b) All this, however, should be regarded as only by way of supplementing other agencies already described. Not many adults, much less boys and girls, reason themselves into a vital faith. For faith, as has already been noted, is a vast deal more than mere belief reached through logical processes. It is vision. It is soul-attitude. It is an immediate experience of spiritual realities. It is trust in and friendship with a living Person. Therefore, one who would help these distraught and bewildered young seekers to attain the kind of assurance they desire must have something more to offer them than proof-texts and syllogisms. The most irresistibly convincing evidence of Christianity is Christ himself. He

149

is "the brightness of the Father's glory and the express image of his person." "He that hath seen me," he said to his disciples, "hath seen the Father also." And one cannot really see God as he is revealed in Jesus and still remain in doubt, however many puzzling questions there may be that he is, as yet, unable to answer. Our primary effort, therefore, should be through personal influence and vital and wisely adapted instruction to bring our boys and girls face to face with him as the surest possible way of establishing them in the faith and enabling them to pass triumphantly through their years of storm and stress and ultimately to find the solution of all their really vital problems.

I venture, however, once more to remind the teacher that, in order that the revelation of Christ may become a vital reality in the life of the youth, he must be given opportunities to express his awakening faith in worship and service. Worship imparts the warmth of life to truth apprehended by the mind, and expression in conduct translates it from the abstract into definite and concrete experience. Doctor Jacob Gould Schurman, in a book written a number of years ago entitled "Agnosticism and Religious Faith," calls attention to the fact that men of action are seldom troubled with religious doubts. The men who are most apt to become skeptical about the fundamental spiritual verities, he says, are those who sit down in closed offices and try to solve the problems of life by processes of reasoning. And his conclusion is that the way to attain religious certitude is by doing rather than by logic. This seems to be in accord with the teaching of Jesus. "If any man," he says, "will do his will, he shall know of the doctrine, whether it be of God, or whether I speak of myself." (John 7: 17.) Many things that seem vague and unreal so long as we simply try to reason them out become clear and real when we begin to translate them into conduct. And if this be true in the case of mature and thoroughly educated men and women, it must be doubly true of boys and girls with their meager information and experience and their limited capacity for abstract thinking.

We should seek, therefore, to beget an intelligent interest on the part of our boys and girls in the great enterprises of the Church and to give them a place in its programs of activity. Our failure at this point has been the occasion of serious loss to the Church in several ways. It has meant failure to utilize the energy and enthusiasm of youth in the great task which we have in hand. It has resulted in the actual loss of many of our youth, who, finding no adequate channels within the Church for the expression of their abounding life, have turned in other directions and have either entirely given up their religious affiliations or have come to regard them as unimportant. And even in the case of those who have continued to maintain a nominal relation to the Church it has in many instances resulted in failure to develop a really virile, capable, and aggressive type of Christian character.

III. Church Membership.

Church membership, if its significance is properly explained, will mean much more to the adolescent than it can possibly mean to the younger boy or girl. And a part of the duty of explaining what it means in the way of ennobling fellowship and of participation in great undertakings in the name of Christ belongs to the Sunday school teacher. By means of such instruction he may not only awaken in those who have been brought into vital fellowship with Christ a real appreciation of the high privilege of being affiliated with those who belong to Christ, but may help to prepare them for entering into the great fellowship. Suggestions in regard to the pastor's part in this preparation will be found in Chapter XII. It may be remarked in passing, however, that what is said there about the importance of making the act of receiving the young into the Church a truly memorable occasion is especially applicable in the case of those who are in the period of early and middle adolescence. For boys and girls of this age are peculiarly responsive both to the profound social implications of such a step and to its sacred symbolic and ceremonial accompaniments. The fine passage quoted from Richter, for instance, could have come only out of the vivid recollection of an adolescent experience, for upon no other would the occasion described have made so deep and vivid an impression.

IV. In Conclusion.

I cannot close this chapter without once more reminding parents, pastors, and teachers of the immense importance of making the most of the unique opportunity that comes with that period in the unfolding life which we are considering. All the conditions of effective appeal through the revelation of Christ are present. Idealism is at its highest, the social nature is in the exuberance of its first awakening, and the soul is stirred by deep religious longings. But these favorable conditions continue at most for only a few years. The high tide of emotional interest, if neglected, soon begins to wane; and the gracious occasion is soon gone, never to return. How important, therefore, that all who are concerned for the future destiny of those who are in the midst of this period of spiritual awakening and eager yearning shall unite in helping them to find in Christ the satisfaction of their deepest needs and in seeking so to establish them in their loyalty and devotion to him that no future temptations can ever lead them to doubt him or to forsake him!

SUGGESTIONS FOR STUDY

1. Try to determine what is meant by the "General Adaptation of Evangelistic Agencies" as explained in this chapter.

2. Consider what this requires (a) in regard to the teacher's personal influence, (b) in regard to the content of instruction, (c) in regard to methods of instruction, and (d) as to forms of service.

3. Discuss the meaning of "Individual Adaptation" as here explained.

4. What do the principles set forth require in regard to the particular adolescent group with which you are dealing?

5. What efforts are you making to apply these principles?

6. Consider what types of conversion experience may be expected of adolescents.

7. Discuss the whole matter of receiving adolescent boys and girls into the Church.

153

CHAPTER X

YOUNG PEOPLE AND ADULTS

IT would be better, if the space at our command were sufficient, to study these two groups separately. Since, however, the fundamental principles and methods which should be adopted in dealing with them are quite similar, it is entirely possible to consider them together.

I. POSSIBILITIES OF THE ORGANIZED CLASS OR DEPARTMENT

There is no other section of the local Church that has in it greater possibilities as an evangelistic agency than the young people's or adult class or department.

1. It furnishes an opportunity for bringing home to men and women in a vital way the truth of God's word. And we must never forget that the word itself, if properly presented and adequately apprehended, has convincing and convicting power. It awakens a vivid realization of moral and spiritual need and reveals Christ as the One in whom alone this need may be satisfied. "The entrance of thy word," sings the Psalmist, "giveth light." (Ps. 119: 130.) In that light we are enabled to see ourselves and to appreciate in some measure the high calling of God in Christ Jesus, and so are led to shame for our shortcomings, to penitence for our sins, and to a sense of dependence upon God for deliverance. St. Paul tells us that "the holy Scriptures are able to make us wise unto salvation

154

through faith which is Christ Jesus" (2 Tim. 3: 15), and that "the gospel is the power of God unto salvation to every one that believeth" (Rom. 1: 16).

It is often assumed that preaching, as the modern Church understands it, is almost the only means of effectively conveying the messages of the sacred writings to the people. Doubtless this assumption is partly the result of a misinterpretation of First Corinthians 1: 21, which in the King James Version reads: "For after that in the wisdom of God the world by wisdom knew not God, it pleased God by the foolishness of preaching to save them that believe." This translation, however, is misleading. The Greek word translated "preaching" has no reference whatever to our modern custom of taking texts and delivering sermons. It means the Christian message and specifically, as the connection shows, the message of the cross, without any reference whatever to the manner of conveying that message to the people. Of course one of the ways of doing so, and perhaps in many cases the most effective way, is by preaching as we now understand the word; but it is not the only way. The message may be taught to individuals or small groups as well as proclaimed to great congregations. Teaching is as definitely provided for in the New Testament as preaching. Our Lord himself was the greatest of teachers as well as the greatest of preachers and is spoken of much more frequently as teacher than as preacher.

It will be seen upon a moment's consideration that there are many reasons why teaching as well as preach-

155

ing should be used as a means for making known the message of life.

(1) It makes possible a vast increase in the evangelistic force of the Church. The gift of real prophetic utterance is quite rare. Only a small per cent of all the millions who are members of the Church could by any possibility become effective preachers. There are very many, however, who, if they should consecrate themselves whole-heartedly to the task, could by study and practice become effective teachers. And this means that teaching offers a way by which a vast multitude of lay members may become useful evangelists.

(2) While preaching has its decided advantages as an evangelistic agency, there are advantages also that belong to teaching.

The teacher may come into a much closer relation with the members of his class than it is possible for the preacher to gain with the members of his congregation, and so may make more effective use of the personal appeal.

Since the group to which the teacher ministers is usually much smaller and more homogeneous than that to which the preacher appeals, it is possible for him to adapt both his message and the manner of presenting it to an extent that is usually impossible for the preacher.

The teacher can present the truth more consecutively and systematically than the preacher.

The teacher, as a rule, uses a textbook and may in many cases secure the personal coöperation of his pupils by encouraging them to study for themselves the things he wishes them to learn.

2. The organized class affords a special opportunity for making the work of the teacher effective by creating a warm atmosphere of Christian brotherhood and by opening up channels of service for the members of the class.

3. The organized class affords unusually favorable opportunities for personal evangelism, or what Doctor H. C. Trumbull speaks of as "individual work for individuals."

II. THE TEACHER'S PART

1. In what is said in the preceding section it is assumed that the organized class has, as a rule, a relatively small membership. I am sure that wherever capable teachers can be secured this is the best plan. An adult or young people's *department* may have as many members as can be induced to join it, but for study it is always best in the former and generally so in the latter that the large department should be broken up into small groups. For most of the advantages mentioned above are very apt to be lost when the class is very large. Personal contact between teacher and pupils and the special adaptation of material and methods become impossible, and the teaching in many cases degenerates into a mere lecture or lay sermon. This lay sermon in most cases is inferior both in content and as to effectiveness of presentation to the sermon preached by the pastor at the regular hour of Sunday worship, and yet not infrequently its most conspicuous result is

157

that it keeps a large number of people away from the stated services of the Church. I have known more than one large Bible class which, instead of helping the pastor, became a positive hindrance to him. If you must try to teach a large class, see, at any rate, that your work supplements that of your pastor instead of making it more difficult. But do not attempt to do so if you can possibly help it. For you will be much more likely to do really vital work with a small, homogeneous group than with a miscellaneous crowd.

2. In a school in which there is a large young people's or adult department division into classes should be upon the basis of interest. The best plan for making such a division is for the superintendent and pastor, after due consultation with the Department Director of Study and Training and the leaders of the organized classes, to secure the services of as many teachers as may be required, ask each teacher to offer one or more courses, and then allow the members of the department and classes to select the courses which they wish to take. If the school is so small that there can be only one young people's and one adult class, the teacher of each should still, after consultation with the members of his class and after a careful study of their needs, select the course which seems to be best adapted to them. In most cases this will be found in either the Uniform or Graded Lessons, but there will be other cases in which some of the Elective Courses approved by the proper authorities of the Church may well be introduced.

3. The best course that can be secured, however,

158

will be ot no avail unless it is effectively taught, and several things are required for effective teaching.

The teacher must set before him certain definite aims determined by a careful study of the personnel of his class. The aim in the case of a part of the membership will be to lead those composing it into closer fellowship with Jesus Christ and to a more adequate understanding of and devotion to Christian ideals of life and conduct. In the case of others it will be to awaken conviction and to lead to repentance and to faith in Christ as a personal Saviour. In both cases the aim is to be accomplished by a vital revelation of the person of Christ and interpretation of his teachings and work; and, whatever lesson courses may be selected, they should be used with this end in view. That is, in all religious teaching Christ must be central as he is central in all the teachings of the Bible. "Ye search the Scriptures," said Jesus to the Pharisees, "because ye think that in them ye have eternal life; and these are they which bear witness of me; and ye will not come to me, that ye may have life." (John 5: 39.) That is, although all the Scriptures center about Christ and bear witness to him, these men failed in their study of the Scriptures to discover him and to find life in him. And it is possible for the modern Bible student to make the same mistake and for the modern Bible teacher to fail so to utilize his Biblical material as to lead his pupils to a definite knowledge of Christ and a saving faith in him.

4. In order that the teacher may avoid this error, it will be necessary for him (1) to seek diligently to come to a clear understanding of the characteristics and

needs of the members of his class, (2) to study carefully the whole body of lesson material with these needs constantly in mind, and (3) to plan his lessons with a view to accomplishing the aims which he has set before him. No one can be a successful teacher of religion who is not an earnest and intelligent student of the Bible and who is unable to come into vital personal relation with those whom he seeks to lead in the way of life.

5. The spirit and personality of the teacher count for quite as much in the case of a class of young people or adults as in the case of a teacher of children or youth. It is futile, therefore, to expect to accomplish the aims which are set forth above under the leadership of one who is not himself deeply in earnest and who is not able through the strength of his personality and the recognized nobility and integrity of his life to command the confidence and respect of his class. This at once suggests a possible explanation of the failure of many Bible classes to become effective evangelistic agencies and the responsibility of pastor and superintendent for seeing that men who know neither Christ nor their Bibles are not selected as teachers in the Sunday school. To be sure, to secure those who are really qualified for this high and sacred task is often difficult and sometimes impossible; but it is at least questionable as to whether or not a class is really worth while if it must be taught by a person whose life and attitudes misrepresent instead of revealing and commending the ideals for which Christianity stands.

III. The Officers

The young people of every Sunday school should be organized into a young people's department and the adults into an adult department. In small schools there may be but one class in each of these departments. In schools in which the enrollment is sufficient there are frequently two classes in each, one for men and another for women. In large schools there ought, as has already been suggested, to be several study groups, the membership of each group being determined on the basis of community of interest. The purpose of departmental organization is to develop a sense of unity and an *esprit de corps* in each group and to enable the various classes in each to coöperate in the carrying out of common or related programs of service. In the small school the class and department officers will be practically the same; but in the school in which there are two or more classes in a department each class should have its own organization, with such officers as its work may require. For plans of organization for departments and classes the reader should write to the General Sunday School Board, 810 Broadway, Nashville, Tenn.

There should be the closest possible coöperation between the officers of each department and the teachers and officers of the various classes in the planning and carrying out of special evangelistic programs, such as the annual evangelistic campaign in the Sunday school and such special evangelistic services as may from time to time be arranged by the pastor. This coöperation should include, among other things, the following:

11   161

(1) Frequent meetings for prayer and consultation.

(2) Community surveys and definite arrangements for bringing in new members and for bringing back those who have temporarily dropped out of the school.

(3) Plans for securing the regular attendance of members at the class sessions and at the Church services during the special evangelistic season.

(4) Provision for individual work with individuals by such members of the class as may be effectively used in this kind of service. A helpful handbook for those who wish to prepare themselves for this kind of service is "Introducing Men to Christ," by W. D. Weatherford.

(5) Planning the services of worship with a view to making them real evangelistic services.

In a school in which there are two or more classes in each department there ought to be, in addition to the coöperative programs arranged by the officers and teachers of each department, a special program by each class in each department. Indeed, a part of the work of the officers and teachers of the department should be the assignment of specific tasks to the various classes that compose it. For there are certain things (such as bringing back members who have dropped out, securing regularity of attendance, and planning for personal efforts by members of the class to lead others either in the class or out of it to surrender their lives to Christ) that can be done more effectively by the class than by the department. In planning for personal work of any kind specific tasks should be assigned to individual members on the ground of their fitness for

162

approaching those whom the class is seeking to win. All details in regard to such work should be arranged by a group composed of the teacher, the class officers, and such others as the teacher and the president may select. The names of those selected for this type of service should not, however, be publicly announced.

IV. THE CLASS

In the preceding suggestions it is assumed that in each of the groups which we are considering the department and the various classes are themselves to be organized and conducted as evangelistic agencies. That is, the members of the classes who are affiliated with the Church should coöperate with the officers and teachers in all their evangelistic efforts. The following may be suggested as some of the ways by which the members may help:

1. *By prompt and regular attendance and by intelligent attention to the courses of study that are from time to time agreed upon.* Members of the class who are not definitely committed to the Christian life are not likely to be profoundly impressed either with the importance of the work of the class or with the value of the lessons taught from week to week, if those who profess to be followers of Christ are manifestly indifferent in regard to both. It is not easy to convince a man of the world of the religious sincerity of a Church member who is not sufficiently interested in the great messages revealed in the Bible to study one lesson a week.

2. *By joining heartily in the services of worship.* The most carefully planned service will prove ineffective

if it is not made a medium for expressing the real emotional attitudes of at least a large proportion of those who are present. The effectiveness of public worship grows largely out of the fact that it is a united act in which the spirit of reverence in each individual is recruited and intensified by the common spirit that pervades the group as a whole.

3. *By creating an atmosphere of friendliness and brotherhood.* Men of all types all over the world respond to the influence of such an atmosphere. There are more hearts than most of us suspect that long for real Christain fellowship. Every pastor knows that one of the most common complaints against the Church by those on the outside is that they find it lacking in the spirit of genuine fraternity. There are doubtless cases in which apparent failure at this point is due to difficulties not readily to be overcome rather than to indifference. It is not easy to know just how far to go in greeting strangers in a great congregation on Sunday morning, and, besides, there are many sincerely devout people who do not believe that the hour of worship should close with a season of miscellaneous greeting and conversation in the house of prayer. None of these difficulties exists, however, in the case of the organized class. The group is relatively small, and it is possible for the members to come into intimate personal relations one with another. Moreover, since there are generally separate classes for men and women, the social distinctions that often prove embarrassing in mixed groups may, under proper leadership, be entirely eliminated. We have known organized classes in which day laborers,

merchants, bankers, and professional men of various types mingled together in the finest spirit of Christian brotherhood and without embarrassment or restraint.

Manifestly such a situation furnishes the most favorable conditions for effective teaching and for personal evangelism. To create such a situation, therefore, should be the constant aim of the leaders in every young people's and every adult department. The task, in many cases, will be difficult and will require patient persistence in prayer and in teaching and guidance. For we may as well frankly face the fact that not infrequently the same social prejudices and the same kind of snobbery exist in the Church that are found on the outside and that many lay members of the Church recognize no obligation on their part to engage in personal evangelism. Where such conditions are found to exist, the department and class leaders must, as a matter of first importance, unite with the pastor in continuous efforts to awaken in the members a true spirit of Christian brotherhood and to bring them to a realization of the fact that the Great Commission was given, not to the apostles alone, but to the whole body of believers, and that it is the duty of every man who knows Christ to seek to lead others into the fellowship of the faith. And along with this process of awakening and of instruction in Christian duty there should go a definite program of training designed to fit those who show themselves ready to respond to the divine call for this special type of service.

4. *By engaging in types of service in which the entire membership of the class may take part.* Any wide-awake

165

class may undertake worthy tasks of various kinds that will command the interest of the unconverted as well as of those who are definitely committed to the Christian life. In some cases it may be a community enterprise such as helping to provide for the needs of some local benevolent institution. In others it may mean participation in the support of some institution belonging to the Church that is doing a kind of work that will appeal to almost any reasonably intelligent and well-meaning man or woman. I chance to be acquainted with one class that has aroused an enthusiastic interest in almost its entire membership in a mission school that is offering exceptional educational opportunities to a large number of boys and girls who otherwise would of necessity grow up in ignorance. Where such work is undertaken, regular reports in regard to what is being accomplished should be made to the class. Besides class enterprises, congenial tasks may often be assigned to individuals or to small groups.

The significance of all this in evangelistic effort has already been explained. Truth becomes vital and convincing when one seriously undertakes to put it into practice. Again and again, as I have taught this lesson to classes, members have interrupted me to tell of cases in which men and women had been led to a saving faith in Christ by being engaged in some form of service. Adults as well as children learn by doing.

V. DECISION

No definite rule can be laid down as to the time and manner of making appeals for definite surrender.

In many instances there should be individual appeals made by members of the class in private. Where such an appeal proves effective, announcement of the fact should be made at the next class session, in order that cordial welcome to the brotherhood of believers may be extended to the new convert.

In any class that is properly conducted and that is pervaded by the true evangelistic spirit there will be occasions when, after seasons of special prayer and preparation, appeals may be made before the department or class as a whole. Such occasions ought to occur at frequent intervals during the year and, of course, should be confidently expected and provided for during seasons of intensive evangelistic effort.

What was said in regard to the types of conversion experience that may be expected of intermediate and senior boys and girls is equally applicable in the case of young people and adults. Good men whose conversion was after the manner of that of Saul of Tarsus are sometimes inclined to insist that everybody else must be converted in the same way. Such insistence, however, is likely to mislead and, in some instances, to prove seriously hurtful. Those who seek to become soul winners cannot too often remind themselves that there is no typical emotional experience that accompanies conversion, and that it is always dangerous to get the mind of a seeker after God set on attaining a certain kind of feeling. It is dangerous, in the first place, because it turns his thoughts away from God and fixes them upon himself, and, in the second place, because a normal person is seldom able to attain any

167

given type of emotion by definitely seeking after it. Feeling is simply one of the results of coming into a right relation with God, and the intensity of it in any given case depends partly on individual temperament and partly on the general atmosphere in which the final decision is reached. The doctrine of the witness of the Spirit has always been central in the teaching of Methodism. But the witness of the Spirit must not be identified with any special type of emotion. It has never been so identified by any of the authoritative teachers of Methodism. John Wesley tells about two girls whom he examined upon a certain occasion with a view to receiving them into the Society. Their experiences, he says, were both quite clear. "But what a contrast," he adds, "between them! Sally Blackburn was all calmness; her look, her speech, her whole carriage, was as sedate as if she had lived three-score years. On the contrary, Peggy was all fire; her eyes sparkled, her very features spoke, her whole face was alive, and she looked as if she was just ready to take wings for heaven." Wesley even refused to insist that every regenerate man must *know* that his sins are forgiven. "When, fifty years ago," he says, "my brother Charles and I, in the simplicity of our hearts, taught the people that unless they *knew* their sins were forgiven they were under the wrath and curse of God, I marvel they did not stone us. The Methodists, I hope, know better now." Wesley believed thoroughly in the possibility of immediate fellowship with God and that the Holy Spirit speaks directly to the hearts of men; but he knew that the inner voice may be variously interpreted and that it is even possible for men to fail entirely to understand it. While, therefore, he maintained that it is the privilege of every man to attain through faith and surrender to God "the peace that passeth understanding," he knew too much about the peculiarities of human nature to make any kind of feeling the test of a man's acceptance with God. To a good man, who was discouraged because he lacked joy, Wesley wrote: "You never learned, either from my conversation or preaching or writing, that holiness consisted in a flow of joy; I constantly told you quite the contrary. I told you it was love, the love of God and our neighbor, the life of God in the soul of man; the mind that was in Christ, enabling us to walk as Christ also walked."

All we need concern ourselves about is that we may be able so to reveal Christ to our fellows as to lead them to turn away from their sins and in trust and love surrender their lives to him. And we should constantly remind those for whose salvation we pray and labor that what is required of them is to make sure of their attitude toward Christ; and if they still show signs of uncertainty, we may direct their attention to some of the practical tests that are given in the New Testament. Take, for instance, such passages as Matthew 7: 16-20; John 13: 34, 35; John 15: 14; 1 John 3: 14-18.

VI. Joining the Church

Having led a man to surrender his life to Christ, our next step should be to induce him to unite with some branch of the Church. For, while joining a

Church is not necessary to one's salvation, one who declines to become a member of some organized body of disciples seldom becomes a vital and useful Christian. For such membership involves at least three things, each of which has an important bearing upon one's steadfastness and development in Christian character. It involves (1) the open and positive committal of one's self to a certain interpretation of the meaning of life and to certain definite standards of character and conduct; (2) affiliation with a great body of men and women animated by the same spirit and cherishing the same ideals and aims; and (3) pledging one's self to unite with others under the guidance and inspiration of the Holy Spirit in building the kingdom of God. Such a relation, therefore, furnishes the most favorable conditions for healthy spiritual growth and increasing efficiency in service.

In early Methodism persons desiring to unite with the Church were required to go through a period of probation before being received into full membership. Perhaps it is well that modern Methodists have given up this custom. I fear, however, that in doing so they have swung to the opposite extreme, and that people are now received into the Church with a degree of carelessness and haste which is hardly in keeping with so serious and important a step. The old probation system was much more than a mere period of testing. It was a season of instruction and nurture and training designed to fit new converts for taking their rightful places in the great brotherhood of believers. And I believe that in a vast majority of cases it would still

170

be better for the pastor, before receiving them, privately to talk and pray with those who apply for Church membership, and, as far as he finds it necessary, to instruct them in regard to the meaning of the vows they are to assume and the relationship into which they are to enter.

SUGGESTIONS FOR STUDY.

1. Consider some of the possibilities of the organized department or class as an evangelistic agency.

2. Do you know of any department or class in which these possibilities are being realized?

3. Discuss the teacher's part in making the class a successful evangelistic agency. Discuss the officers' part.

4. How may the class itself help?

5. Discuss the best ways and occasions for making definite appeals for surrender to Christ.

6. Discuss types of conversion experience.

7. Discuss the meaning of the witness of the Spirit.

8. What preparation should be made for receiving young people and adults into the Church?

CHAPTER XI

SPECIAL SEASONS OF EVANGELISM

THE evangelistic work of the Sunday school should not be limited to set occasions and special seasons, but should continue without interruption throughout the entire year. For its aim, as we have agreed, is twofold—namely, by a process that is fundamentally educational (1) to lead children and youth and men and women into vital fellowship through faith with Jesus Christ; and (2) to help those who already know and love Christ to know him better, grow more like him, and serve him more efficiently. It is manifest, therefore, that any cessation in the prosecution of either section of this task must necessarily result in loss. If we are seeking through a wise use of the agencies previously considered to lead a group of pupils to the point of readiness to surrender their lives to Christ, it is folly either to work spasmodically or to wait for some set time at which the process is expected to culminate. On the contrary, our efforts and our prayers should be without ceasing, and we should be always on the lookout for the opportune moment to bring each one of them to a definite decision. And the same kind of continuous effort is required for promoting the religious development of those who already belong to Christ.

I. WHY SPECIAL SEASONS OF EVANGELISM ARE NEEDED

But however faithful and diligent the officers and teachers of a Sunday school may be, there will be need for designated seasons in which special attention shall be given to evangelism in the sense of seeking to bring

172

pupils into conscious fellowship with Christ. The reasons which lie back of this need are quite similar to those suggested in explaining in a former chapter the place of the revival. They may, therefore, be dealt with here very briefly. They grow partly out of our common human limitations and partly out of certain general conditions which it is impossible greatly to change.

1. In order that evangelistic effort may be most effective, it must be shot through with an intensity of passion which it is difficult for even the most devoted follower of Christ, who must necessarily engage in a wide variety of diverting and distracting employments, to maintain continuously. This statement is not to be construed as suggesting that seasons of coldness and indifference are inevitable in the average Christian life. One who knows Christ and is a partaker through faith of the divine nature will be unceasing in his interest in his fellows and in his efforts to bring them to a knowledge of Christ. And yet it may be possible for him occasionally so to arrange his affairs as to be able for a limited time to give such undivided attention to such efforts as will raise his interest to an unusual height of emotional fervor. This is perhaps one of the secrets of what are spoken of in the Bible as "seasons of refreshing from the presence of the Lord."

2. The special evangelistic season should mean unusual effort as well as unusual zeal. In other words, the most effective evangelism calls for an amount of personal work which the average Sunday school teacher, because of his manifold duties and his physical limita-

173

tions, finds it impossible to undertake for more than a few weeks during each year.

3. While the evangelistic aim, interpreted in the broadest sense, should run through all teaching in the Sunday school, much material must necessarily be used which is only indirectly related to the purpose of leading pupils to a positive and definite committal of their lives to Christ. Ideally the lessons to be used during a special evangelistic campaign should be selected with a view to their particular adaptation to the ends which the school is seeking to accomplish. Where this is impossible, however, such supplemental material should be introduced as will enable the teacher clearly and forcefully to present to his pupils the claims of Christ upon the individual, what it means to become a Christian, and the need for immediate positive decision. Such material should, of course, be so graded as to meet the needs of pupils of various types and ages. That is, in the case of those under thirteen or fourteen it should be predominantly positive, consisting mainly of such an interpretation of Christ as will awaken the faith and love and allegiance of boys and girls. In the case of those who are older, there may well be added to similar adapted interpretations pictures of the hideousness and danger of sin and the necessity of repentance and voluntary surrender to Christ as Lord and Saviour.

II. GENERAL SUGGESTIONS

The time and length and manner of conducting the special evangelistic campaign are to be determined in the light of local conditions.

The following recommendations by the General Sunday School Board are especially applicable to town and city schools:

"That three months of the year, or three periods in consecutive order, be devoted as follows to evangelism in the Sunday school: That the first month or period be given to the preparation of the forces, the training of teachers and other Sunday school workers in mind and spirit for the work of evangelists; that the second month or period be given to active evangelism in the Sunday school, in the classes, and by personal effort, this period culminating with Confession or Decision Day; and that the third month or period be given to special preparation of pupils for reception into Church membership.

"The Board suggests that the program begin with January as the month of the preparation of the forces; that February be devoted to the active evangelistic campaign, leading up to Decision or Confession Day; and that the remainder of the time before Easter be used for the careful preparation of those who are to be received into Church membership on Easter Sunday.

"This plan is intended to be suggestive only and is, of course, subject to such modifications as regards the months indicated and minor details as practical considerations may demand. However, the three lines of emphasis represented by the three periods as indicated are regarded as essential to the best and most abiding results."

In a leaflet entitled "A Practical Plan of Sunday School Evangelism" Doctor J. W. Shackford, General

Secretary of the Sunday School Board, offers the following suggestions as to the manner of carrying out these recommendations:

"1. *Period of Preparation of the Forces.*—A special season of evangelistic effort with the Sunday schools ought not to be entered into without careful and prayerful preparation. No school has a right to deal with this supremely important work in a hurried and incidental fashion.

"If this occasion is to have any deep spiritual significance to the pupils of the school, if the purpose is to bring them to Jesus Christ as their Saviour and Friend and to encourage and strengthen the faith and love of those who already are of the kingdom, then the school, with its pastor in the lead and with its entire working force, will spare no pains to make ready the conditions for an evangelism that is vital, normal, and considerate of the religious needs of every pupil in the school.

"Such preparation cannot be had without paying the price. So long as the pastor or teachers think of this work other than as of central importance in the year's program of work, so long will other matters crowd out the program necessary to prepare the forces that are dealing with the young life of the Church.

"This program of planning will involve several things which may here be enumerated briefly:

(1) ORGANIZATION

"Organization involves the definite location of responsibility and clearly defined plans of work. At the beginning of the campaign there should be appointed a *Committee on Evangelism*. This committee should, as a rule, be composed of the pastor, the superintendent, and the superintendents of the organized departments of the school above the primary, or in schools not departmentally organized, one representative teacher of pupils under twelve, one of pupils twelve to seventeen, and one of pupils eighteen years old and over. The duties of this committee will be to plan and promote the program of evangelism in the Sunday school and to supervise and stimulate evangelism throughout the year.

"Copies of leaflet studies on evangelism provided by the General Sunday School Board should be procured in advance with a view to use in connection with the prayer and study conferences to follow. A series of four or five such meetings will be needed for the most thorough preparation both of the teachers and officers themselves and of the plans for a vital and thoroughgoing evangelistic effort in the school. Where for any reason these study conferences are not held the entire series of leaflets should be read by the teachers and officers.

(2) PRAYER AND STUDY CONFERENCES

"The entire working force of the Sunday school, under the leadership of the pastor, will come together in a series of midweek meetings for prayer and conference regarding all that is involved in this vital program of Sunday school evangelism. This will include a consideration of the essential aims of the Sunday school, the meaning of the Christian life, and a study of the religious needs of the pupils both of the classified groups that make up the school membership and of the individuals that compose the groups. It will involve the prayerful consideration of the obligations of the school for these pupils, and it will embrace a study of the best and most intelligent means of meeting their religious needs. It will mean nothing less than an effort to prepare the officers and teachers of the school to become personal evangelists in the best sense.

"This series of conferences will afford the pastor his supreme opportunity to inspire, to train, and to organize the evangelistic forces of the school. Here he will make his officers and teachers understand that he relies upon them as coevangelists with himself in this undertaking. Out of his own experience he will help them to learn how to become effective evangelists.

"Above all, he will lead them in heart-searching prayer that they, as living witnesses to the truth, may guide aright the feet of the young. He will lead them in intercessory prayer that each member of the school may come into the fellowship of Christ and that none who is his may fall away.

(3) DISCOVERING THE SITUATION

"During this period of preparation there should be prepared a careful report on the religious needs of the pupils in all the classes above the primary. These reports should be in the hands of the pastor and the committee before the close of the first period. They will help to bring to the entire group a concrete and definite indication of the scope of the field of immediate responsibility and will suggest where the emphasis needs to be laid and what the wise approach is in each instance.*

(4) PLANNING THE CAMPAIGN

"As the period of preparation draws to a close, the Committee on Evangelism should be prepared to submit a well-thought-out plan for a four weeks' campaign of evangelism in the Sunday school. The plan should be submitted to the whole body of teachers and officers for discussion and for modification, if necessary. The committee should be ready to make announcement of the complete plan by the opening of the second period, the period of active personal and class evangelism.

"2. *Period of Active Evangelism in the Sunday School.* —It is proposed that the month of February be devoted, in special effort in the classes and through personal interviews, to emphasizing the supremacy of Christ for every life and to helping members of the school who have not already entered into the experience of the Christian life to do so at this time. This will be an occasion for the studying of each individual member of the school with a view to giving each just the help needed—to encouraging the pupils who are of the kingdom, to strengthening the weak, to lifting up the fallen, and to seeking and saving those that are lost. It will be a time of personal evangelism of the best sort, and all true evangelism is largely personal. It implies dealing face to face with each individual and helping

*For Report Cards write to the General Sunday School Board, 810 Broadway, Nashville, Tenn.

each in his relations to God. Both in the class and through private interviews there will be opportunities for direct sympathetic personal approach.

(1) COMMITTEES IN THE CLASSES

"A committee on personal evangelism should be appointed in each class of adults and of young people wherever a wise committee of earnest Christian workers is available. Usually the teacher should be the chairman of the committee. In any case, the teacher will keep in close touch with the committee and will actively assist in its work. These committees will undertake through personal work to lead their fellow class members into a definite religious experience through the acceptance of Jesus Christ as Saviour and Lord. Every member of the class who is not known to be a Christian should be interviewed by some earnest member of the class, in each case by the one who is best suited to make the approach.

"Also in the Senior Department a committee will be appointed in each class where, in the judgment of the teacher and the Committee on Evangelism, a suitable committee can be found within the class. The work of this group should be under the direct supervision and guidance of the teacher.

(2) THE WORK OF THE TEACHERS

"During this active campaign the teachers will speak to their classes and seek personal interviews with their pupils on the subject of the Christian life. The wise teacher will make an approach that is tactful, sympathetic, and adapted to the special needs of the pupil. In case especially of junior and intermediate children the teachers will visit the homes in order to assist parents in throwing helpful influences around the children, so that their religious quickening and decision for Christ may have the fullest significance and the most abiding results in their lives.

(3) COÖPERATION OF THE PARENTS

"The work of Sunday school evangelism will fail in large measure if the parents of the children are not closely related to this work. Nothing is more important in a campaign of this sort than that the parents be brought into closest sympathy with the awakening religious interests of their children and that they be prepared to help them with their counsel and their prayers. To this end, both by communications sent to the parents and by personal visitation, every effort should be made to bring about the fullest coöperation in the homes.

(4) THE PASTOR'S ASSISTANCE

"During the campaign, in the departments and classes, or before the entire school where the school assembles in one room, the pastor, or some one whom the pastor may select as especially qualified, will make brief, simple talks on the meaning of the Christian life. In these talks earnest emphasis should be laid upon the fact that the school desires all its members to have a personal, living faith in Christ.

"The effort should be made to explain very simply what it means to be a Christian and what is involved in making public confession of Christ. It should be made very clear that there are some who already love the Saviour, but who have not yet confessed him publicly; that there may be others who have not given their hearts to him, but who ought to do so at this time, and that there is no reason to wait for any particular day or season.

"During this campaign the pastor will give re-enforcement from the pulpit. He will preach to the teachers and working forces in the Church and Sunday school. He will deliver at least one sermon to the parents which they will be especially invited to hear. Not only will he point out the responsibility of the parents for leading their children to Christ, but he will also help to remove some of the difficulties which often exist in the minds of the parents and prevent them from encouraging their children in their religious life.

(5) CONTINUED MEETINGS OF WORKERS

"During the campaign there will still be need for weekly meetings of officers and teachers, at which there should be brief reports of developments and a consideration of the problems that arise in connection with the campaign. It should be remembered that some of the teachers will be without experience in trying to do the work expected of them. Many of them will meet with difficulties that they do not know how to overcome. These matters should have careful consideration, and help should be given as far as possible in each instance. Also reports of encouraging experiences should be made for the inspiration that this will give.

(6) REACHING BEYOND THE SCHOOL

"The quickened interest in the personal salvation of others is apt to enlarge the sense of responsibility of the workers in the school for those on the outside as well as for those within the school. There are always some who, through personal relations with the members of the class or because of former membership in the school, are more or less a part of that company for which the teacher and the class are responsible. In this work, therefore, effort should be made to win for Christ all those upon whom the school has even an indirect hold."

In the southern section of our territory the first part of the year will in many cases be found to be quite as suitable a time for a special evangelistic season in rural communities as in towns and cities. Farther north, where the weather is likely to be inclement during the winter, it will often be best to select some other season. Since there are distinct advantages in a simultaneous campaign extending as widely as possible, it might be well for each Annual Conference to recommend some period to be observed as far as possible by all its rural charges. It will generally be found expedient to make the campaign in the country considerably shorter than the time suggested for town and city.

Whenever and wherever a special season of evangelism is observed, it ought to be immediately preceded by a systematic effort to bring in new members, to the end that as many individuals as possible may be brought under its influence.

III. DECISION DAY

The special season should culminate on a day agreed upon and announced several weeks in advance. The name most commonly used to designate this occasion is "Decision Day." For obvious reasons this designation is seriously objectionable. "Confession Day" has been suggested as a substitute; but the word "confession" in ecclesiastical parlance carries with it certain associations which make it a bit offensive to the ears of Protestant Christians. The name, however, does not greatly matter, provided we fully understand for what the occasion stands. It should be clearly explained that the setting apart of a certain day as marking the culmination of the evangelistic campaign does not mean either that teachers are to postpone all definite efforts to lead their pupils to surrender their lives to Christ or that the pupils should postpone their surrender until the fixed day arrives. On the contrary, the teachers should understand that they are expected to be constantly praying and working for the salvation of their pupils and constantly seeking to impress upon them the fact that the time for decision is not to-morrow or next week or next month, but this very hour. In other words, the day should be thought of by all rather as a time when public confession of Christian discipleship is to be made than as a time when persons are to be urged to accept Christ as Lord and Saviour.

The work suggested above is all a part of the preparation for Decision Day, and throughout its progress frequent mention should be made of the occasion in the teachers' meetings and before the school and the various departments and classes, care being taken always to guard against such misunderstanding as is referred to above. There are other items in the preparation, however, which require careful attention.

1. *Full attendance of teachers and pupils.* Diligent effort should be made to secure a full attendance of both teachers and pupils.

Pastor, superintendent, and other leaders should earnestly seek to develop such a spirit in the working force of the school as will make it impossible for any member of the force to absent himself from the service except under conditions that render it impossible for him to attend.

In order to make sure of a full attendance of pupils, the coöperation of parents, interested members of the classes, and members of the congregation should be enlisted. Teachers should visit the homes of their pupils, explain to the parents the significance of the day, and seek to impress them with the importance of seeing that their children are present. In departments above the junior, pupils who are already Christians may not infrequently be charged with the responsibility of looking after the attendance of those about whom there is doubt. And in many cases members of the Church may be found who will volunteer to bring in their cars pupils who are so situated that it requires considerable effort for them to reach the church.

2. *Attendance of parents and other friends.* The agencies suggested above should also be employed for bringing to the service the parents of the pupils and such

185

other friends from the outside as are within reach. The latter will naturally include some who were once members of the Sunday school and others who are related to it through their family connections or personal friendships. Especially important is it, however, to secure the attendance of as many of the parents of pupils as possible, since their presence will not only increase the importance of the occasion in the estimation of their children, but will, if properly conducted, prove a blessing also to the parents themselves.

3. *Program.* The program for the day should be carefully planned in advance, and both individuals and classes should be definitely instructed as to what parts they will be expected to take. The planning should include the selection and practice of hymns and the arrangement of the entire order of service. The following outline is merely suggestive and may be modified as conditions require:

(1) 9:30 to 10:00 A.M. Devotional service in each of the several departments or in the school as a whole. The utmost care should be taken to see that these services are really devotional. Appropriate hymns with which the pupils are familiar should be selected in advance, and the prayers should be short and should deal directly with the matter that is uppermost in the minds of those present. If the service is held for the entire school, a brief, simple talk should be made by the pastor or superintendent. If separate services are held in the various departments, a talk should be made in each either by the department superintendent or by some teacher selected with a view to his special fitness

186

for the task. At the close of the service or services the regular weekly offering should be taken and records of attendance made.

(2) 10:00 to 10:20 A.M. Meeting of the teachers with their classes for brief talks in regard to the meaning of the day. In these talks each teacher should seek to explain in terms that are adapted to the understanding and experiences of his pupils what it means to be a Christian and why every one should become a follower of Jesus. If conditions seem to be propitious, it may be well at the close of the service to give an opportunity to any one who is ready to do so to make a confession of Christ before the class. If cards are used, those who accept the invitation and any who have already made their decisions but have not announced them should be given an opportunity to sign the cards. The class session should close with another brief season of prayer.

(3) 10:20 to 10:50 A.M. Public confession service. In the small school this service should include the entire membership above the Primary Department. In the departmentally organized school it will generally be found best to hold the confession service for the Junior Department apart from the remainder of the school.

The main service should be held in the auditorium, the teachers being seated with their respective classes. The service should include a number of appropriate hymns, a number of brief prayers by persons selected and notified in advance and a carefully prepared talk of ten or fifteen minutes by the pastor. In this talk the pastor should present once more in fresh and vital terms the call of Christ and what this call involves. If the pupils have been wisely taught during the preceding weeks, there will be no need for the kind of emotional appeal that is often found necessary in dealing with adults. The pastor should keep constantly in mind the facts in regard to child life which have been presented in previous chapters and should carefully avoid any appeal that is based on experiences that are necessarily foreign to childhood and youth. The young heart, as a rule, is still tender and responsive, and all that is needed is such a presentation of Christ and his ideal as will answer to the spiritual needs of boys and girls, followed by an earnest, simple invitation to accept Christ and openly and positively to declare their allegiance to him and their purpose to follow and serve him.

After the talk the pastor may ask those who belong to Christ and are already members of the Church to stand. While these remain standing, an invitation may be given to those who have accepted Christ, but have not yet united with the Church, to stand with them. Those who accept this invitation may then be requested to come forward and take their stand about the altar, and while they remain in this position those who desire to begin the Christian life at once may be tenderly urged to come and take their places with them. The pastor must be his own judge as to how far this appeal is to be pressed and what length of time is to be devoted to it. The appeal should be followed by an altar service in which prayer is offered for those who have already accepted Christ that they may, like the Boy of Nazareth, increase in wisdom and in favor with God and man as they increase in stature, and for those who have not yet done so that they may now fully and completely surrender their hearts to him. Immediately after this prayer an opportunity should be given to such as have made the decision to declare it by giving their hands to the pastor.

The altar service over, the pastor should explain briefly why followers of Christ should belong to some branch of the Church and should give an opportunity to all who have come forward to express their desire to unite with the Church. He should explain, however, the reasons why they will not be received at once—that it will be necessary in the case of the boys and girls to consult with their parents and that all will need further instruction in regard to the meaning of the vows they will be required to assume and the new relationship into which they are to enter.

The service should close with a song in which the notes of thanksgiving and gladness and triumph are conspicuous.

IV. After Decision Day

1. The first business of the pastor after Decision Day will be to visit the parents of children who have applied for membership in the Church and seek, not only to gain their consent to the step which their children desire to take, but also to enlist their intelligent interest and whole-hearted encouragement. In some instances opposition, which will require tactful handling, will be

encountered. Parents will object to their children joining the Church, not because they do not want them to be Christians, but because their minds are filled with erroneous notions in regard to the religious possibilities of childhood, the way in which the religious life of the child begins and the process by which the babe in Christ may be brought to the fullness of Christian manhood or womanhood. A careful rereading of the previous chapters of this book will furnish suggestions as to how these objections are to be met. In case the parents of any child refuse to surrender their objection, the utmost pains should be taken to prevent the child from becoming discouraged and deciding that it is not worth while for him to make further effort to live the Christian life. Perhaps it might be well for the pastor to tell him that he will enter his name in a book kept especially for those who are candidates for Church membership and that meanwhile, if he will continue to pray for God's help and to do his best to live as a loyal friend of Jesus, he will have a right to partake with other Christians of the sacrament of the Lord's Supper. Such assurances, however, will amount to but little unless they are followed by intimate personal attention and wise guidance on the part of both pastor and teacher. The situation of the child who finds his sincere religious aspirations thwarted by those to whom he has a right to look for encouragement and support is exceedingly disheartening and calls for the utmost tact and sympathy on the part of those who seek to hold him steadfast in his purpose.

2. Having come to an understanding with the parents

of the children who wish to be received into the Church, the pastor should next address himself to the task of preparing applicants of all ages for the step they are about to take through a definite course of instruction in regard to the meaning of the vows which they are to assume and the fellowship into which they are to enter. Suggestions in regard to the importance of this preparation and what it should include will be given in the next chapter.

SUGGESTIONS FOR STUDY

1. Give three reasons why special evangelistic seasons in the Sunday school are necessary.

2. Discuss the program for an evangelistic campaign suggested by Doctor Shackford.

3. What modifications of this program would be required to adapt it to your local Church and community?

4. Discuss the suggestive program for Decision Day and consider how it might be improved.

5. How would you deal with parents who objected to their children joining the Church on the ground that they were too young to understand what they were doing?

6. How would you deal with a child whose parents refused to give their consent to his joining the Church?

CHAPTER XII

A COÖPERATIVE TASK

THE task of making a Sunday school an effective evangelistic agency is one which calls for intelligent and harmonious coöperation on the part of all who are related to it.

I. COÖPERATION BETWEEN OFFICERS AND TEACHERS

There must be coöperation between the officers and teachers. To the suggestions in regard to plans for working together which have been given in previous chapters, the following may be added:

1. They must be "of one heart and one soul" (Acts 4: 32) and must "have the mind in them which was also in Christ Jesus" (Phil. 2: 5–8). That is, they must be united in the bonds of Christian brotherhood and dominated by the spirit of self-sacrificing service. For without such unity of heart and purpose it will be impossible for them to create the kind of religious atmosphere which is absolutely necessary for the spiritual awakening and development of boys and girls. The officers and teachers of every Sunday school should have occasional meetings devoted largely, if not exclusively, to prayer to the end that they may be able to keep "the unity of the Spirit in the bond of peace." (Eph. 4: 3.) Into these meetings brief seasons of testimony may occasionally be profitably introduced. Some schools have adopted the custom of having the workers assemble each Sunday morning in a quiet room for a

brief period of worship before going into the school session. This has the advantage of putting each one into a frame of mind and heart that is in keeping with the work of the day.

The workers must be of one mind also in the sense of having a common understanding of the nature and a common appreciation of the importance of their evangelistic task. Every teacher should think of himself as an evangelist and of his work as an adventure in the making and training of disciples and should "give diligence to show himself approved unto God, a workman needing not to be ashamed." One half-hearted and indifferent teacher may diminish the spiritual fervor and hinder the work of an entire group of consecrated men and women.

2. They must, however, think and plan together as well as pray together. No Sunday school can be really successful without an intelligently conducted Workers' Council, in which matters relating to the work of each teacher as well as to the school as a whole are carefully considered. The following are some of the matters which may be taken up in these meetings:

(1) Looking after absentees and those who have become irregular in their attendance.

(2) Consideration of the best ways of dealing with pupils who are difficult to understand or to manage.

(3) Exchanges of opinion in regard to helpful articles, pamphlets, and books.

(4) Discussion in regard to pictures and music that may be profitably used in the school and in regard to the planning of effective devotional services.

13   193

(5) Plans for special seasons and special days, such as the revival, the evangelistic campaign, Decision Day, Rally Day, etc.

(6) Plans for community visitation and for visiting the homes of pupils.

II. COÖPERATION BETWEEN THE SUNDAY SCHOOL AND THE HOME

Frequent references have been made during this course of studies to the need for coöperation between the home and the Sunday school. The matter is of sufficient importance, however, to justify further study.

There was a time when Sunday school workers naïvely assumed that they were quite sufficient for the task of bringing up boys and girls in the nurture and admonition of the Lord without the help of their fathers and mothers. No intelligent Sunday school worker to-day, however, would think of committing himself to any such position. For it is now universally admitted, not only that the home may be by far the most effective school of religion in the world, but also that without the help of the home the work of the Sunday school becomes exceedingly difficult. For the influence of an indifferent or irreligious home may effectively counteract all the efforts of the most faithful and consecrated group of Sunday school workers. Perhaps the most discouraging aspect of our task of evangelism in the Sunday school is the decline of home training. I read an article a few years ago by an elderly preacher in which the author stated that in his boyhood ninety-nine per cent of Methodist parents had regular family

194

worship in their homes, but that he had lived to see the time when not more than one per cent did so. Perhaps the former of these statements may have been somewhat exaggerated; and let us hope, at any rate, that the percentage mentioned in the latter is too small. But that there has been a sad decline in family worship during the last fifty years there can be no question.

These considerations at once suggest that to secure the intelligent and faithful coöperation of fathers and mothers is an important part of the work of the Sunday school, and that it is so regarded by our Sunday school leaders is made evident by the earnest attention which they are giving to the matter. Witness, for instance, the organization and development of the Parent-Teacher Association in the Sunday school as an integral part of the work of our General Sunday School Board. One of the leaflets dealing with this Association, which is issued by the Board, contains the following introductory statement:

"The modern Sunday school is endeavoring to promote a systematic and adequate program of religious education for the child, the youth, and the adult. It is clearly recognized by those who are responsible for this program that, no matter how efficient the Sunday school may be, it cannot take the place of the home. It is realized also that the best work in the Sunday school can be accomplished only when there is the fullest understanding and sympathy between the home and the Sunday school. There is a mutual need, a mutual task, a mutual responsibility. It is necessary

195

that the parents and the teachers shall meet in conference to talk over the problems facing them and to plan how the parents in the home may supplement and complete the task of the Sunday school teacher as he promotes the program of the Sunday school."

The means which the Sunday school may employ to secure the coöperation of the home and to make such coöperation increasingly effective may be summarized as follows:

1. I have had occasion again and again to call attention to the fact that no one can successfully teach a Sunday school class who is not acquainted with the home life of his pupils, and I have urged this as a reason why the teacher should systematically visit their homes. There is, however, another reason for his doing so. It is very important that the teacher should establish relations of personal friendship with the fathers and mothers of his pupils in order that he may give them a clear understanding of what he is seeking to do for their children and may secure their intelligent support. The very fact that a child understands that his parents are deeply and vitally interested in the work of the Sunday school will tend to increase his estimate of its value and his interest in and respect for it. Besides this, however, parents who, through frequent conferences with the teachers of their children, come to an intelligent understanding of what the Sunday school is seeking to accomplish may render invaluable service by seeing that their children are regular and prompt in their attendance, by assisting them in the preparation of their lessons, and by recruiting the work of the school

through their personal interest and influence. Every Sunday school teacher, therefore, should seek to become a recognized friend in the homes of all the members of his class, and to this end should not only visit these homes from time to time for the purpose of talking with the parents about their children, but should give special attention to them on those occasions when such attention will be likely to be especially appreciated, such, for instance, as in times of trouble or in times of special rejoicing and thanksgiving.

Effective visitation requires a kind of tact which every teacher should seek diligently to acquire. It must have in it no air of professionalism. If the home visited is one of wealth and high social standing, the teacher should go without apology, assuming that his task is sufficiently dignified and important to command the respect of the most cultured. If it is a home of poverty, he should enter it without affectation or appearance of condescension, seeking to make clear the fact that he wishes to be recognized simply as a friend who desires for friendship's sake to become more intimately acquainted with both parents and children. In these visits the teacher will, of course, talk about the plans and work of the Sunday school, the lessons which the children are studying, and the activities in which he is seeking to engage them. He will not forget to mention any good qualities that the children may possess or anything in their conduct and deportment which is deserving of commendation; and at the same time, if there are points at which they are falling short, he will seek in a kindly and tactful way to bring them

197

to the attention of the parents and to suggest ways in which they may assist in bringing about the improvements that are desired.

2. The school should send regular reports to parents in regard to the attendance and work of their children.

3. Frequent meetings between groups of teachers and parents should be held for the discussion of common problems and the best ways of solving them. Programs for these meetings should be carefully prepared in advance and definite assignments made to those who are expected to take part in them.

4. Wherever it is possible, parents' classes should be organized both for Bible study and for the study of child nature and child training.

5. Parents should be definitely informed in regard to all special evangelistic efforts in the Sunday school, and suggestions should be offered as to how they may help in making these efforts effective.

6. Mention is made above of the work of the Parent-Teacher Association. Such an association should, if possible, be organized in every congregation. Leaflets explaining the various departments of the work of the Association and offering suggestions as to methods for carrying on this work will be furnished upon application to the General Sunday School Board. By a careful study of these leaflets officers and teachers of Sunday schools in which Parent-Teacher Associations have not been organized may obtain valuable suggestions as to how they may keep in close and vital touch with the parents of their pupils, to the end that they may aid

them in preparing for their sacred responsibility and may secure their hearty and intelligent coöperation.

In spite of all that modern writers of neurotic fiction say about the increasing desire on the part of parents for emancipation from exacting home duties, it is quite certain that most parents still love their children and desire to see them properly brought up. The trouble is, however, that many of them do not realize how largely responsible they themselves are for determining the future destiny of their children, and many of those who have some vague realization of this responsibility do not know how to meet it. The task of the Sunday school in relation to such parents, therefore, is twofold: First to awaken within them a real interest in the religious education of their children, and then to help them to make definite and intelligent preparation for this sacred task. There will be but few instances in which Sunday school pupils drawn from homes in which this effort has been successfully carried out may not be won to a living faith in Christ and brought into fellowship with the Church.

III. The Entire Church

The Sunday school does not belong exclusively to the small group of men and women who make up its corps of officers and teachers. It is the great organized agency of the Church for promoting educational evangelism in the broad sense in which the term is used in these studies. It deserves, therefore, the united support of the entire congregation.

The Discipline of our Church designates "the Quar-

199

terly Conference of each circuit and station as a Board of Managers, having charge of all the Sunday schools within its bounds," and makes it "the duty of the Quarterly Conference to keep itself informed as to the condition and needs of the Sunday schools under its care and to see that they are furnished with all necessary equipment." If Quarterly Conferences throughout the Church should begin generally to take this responsibility seriously, there would come about a rapid improvement in the quality of our Sunday school work. For it would not only mean better equipment for Sunday schools in the way of buildings, literature, and other needed helps; but would put new heart into officers and teachers and beget in both pupils and Church members a deeper appreciation of the work which the Sunday school is seeking to accomplish.

The Quarterly Conference, however, should not be content with furnishing the Sunday school with material equipment, but should seek also by sympathetic coöperation to promote its spiritual objectives. The members of the Conference should be members of the school and should assist personally in making effective its evangelistic ministry.

Finally the Conference should join heartily with the pastor in continuous efforts to bring the entire membership of the Church to an adequate understanding and appreciation of the evangelistic mission of the Sunday school and to a common purpose to create an atmosphere that is favorable to the carrying out of a vital evangelistic program. In other words, the ideal which every congregation should keep constantly before it should be the entire membership focalizing attention upon one great central aim.

IV. THE PLACE OF THE PASTOR

Every great coöperative task must have a unifying and directing head. And in the Sunday school this head must in most cases be the pastor. There is doubtless an occasional instance in which a layman has sufficient interest and training and influence in the community to enable him largely to relieve the pastor of the burden of leadership in the Sunday school. Such cases, however, are comparatively rare, and it is not at all certain that it is ever best for a pastor to commit to other hands, however capable they may be, the entire responsibility for the direction of the work of educational evangelism in his congregation. What we are mainly concerned about here, however, is that vast multitude of schools in which there is not likely to be any effective leadership if it is not supplied by the pastor.

1. The fundamental condition of success in the pastoral leadership of the Sunday school is that the pastor himself shall be deeply interested in the work which the Sunday school is set to accomplish and that he shall be thoroughly familiar with educational principles and methods. For he cannot awaken an interest on the part of teachers and parents in an undertaking in which he himself is not interested, nor can he become the effective leader of an enterprise with the scope and aim and demands of which he is not thoroughly familiar. One of the most encouraging facts connected with our

201

present-day Sunday school work is that a large number of our pastors are taking our courses in Leadership Training and thus seeking to fit themselves for effectively guiding the work of educational evangelism and training in their charges.

2. The following suggestions may be offered as to some of the ways by which the pastor may become an influential factor in the development and success of his Sunday school:

(1) He may preach often on some phase of religious education. Pastors frequently find it necessary to preach on subjects which they know will appeal to only a small section of their congregations. But the subject of Christian nurture in its relation to the destiny of the individual, the building of the kingdom of God, and the preservation and development of civilization, if properly presented, will make a well-nigh universal appeal. For all right-minded men and women of every age and station are interested in children themselves, and most of them are interested in preserving for future generations the priceless spiritual inheritance which has been bequeathed to us through the labors and sacrifices of those who have gone before us. The pastor, therefore, who is able to speak with conviction and authority can always count on a vital response to any message which concerns itself with the saving of civilization by the Christian nurture and training of the young.

Through these sermons and through private personal interviews the pastor should seek to make clear to parents their responsibility for the religious training of their children. "Many a parent," says Doctor J.

202

W. Shackford in a leaflet on "The Home and the Sunday School in Christian Evangelism," issued by the General Sunday School Board, "is utterly ignorant as to the extent to which the child's ideals, sentiments, and attitudes are being predetermined without the child's knowledge or choice. Parents talk of the age of accountability when the child will make its own decisions, but they fail to recognize that whenever the child shall arrive at that age it will usually find itself already in possession of certain very definite religious attitudes, habits, and character, which are always in large measure, if not entirely, the result of the decisions which others have made for him." That is, the child's choices are largely predetermined for him by the influences brought to bear upon his life in the home. There are some homes so vitally Christian that it is almost certain that children who grow up in them will from the beginning give their hearts in love and trust to Jesus Christ. In other words, they are really "brought up in the nurture and admonition of the Lord," and are ready to be formally recognized as members of the Church as soon as they are able to understand what Church membership means.

(2) In the Methodist Episcopal Church, South, it is the pastor's duty to nominate to the Quarterly Conference the person who is to act as Sunday school superintendent, and there is no way in which he can contribute more directly to the evangelistic success of the school than by giving to this duty the most prayerful and serious attention. No Sunday school with an indifferent and inefficient superintendent can be really

effective in making and training disciples. On the other hand, a Sunday school with the most meager equipment may accomplish wonders under the guidance of a superintendent who is studious, open-minded, and vitally religious and who has the gift of leadership, ability to work harmoniously with others, and real love for and interest in the task in which he is engaged. If no such person can be found among the adult members of the congregation, the pastor should seek to discover some young man who has in him the making of a successful superintendent and, having found him, should proceed as rapidly as possible to train him for the work.

(3) The pastor should seek to maintain the closest possible intimacy with his staff of Sunday school officers and teachers. He should attend and take part in the deliberations of the Workers' Council, not only that he may keep the Council from making mistakes, but also that he may aid in the development of plans for larger and more effective work.

He should seek to inspire the officers and teachers with the evangelistic passion, to bring them to an increasing understanding and appreciation of the place of religious education in the evangelistic program of the Church, to awaken them to an adequate realization of the need for definite preparation for their work, and to make it possible for them to acquire such preparation.

(4) He should seek to enlist the intelligent interest of the Quarterly Conference in the Sunday school, to the end that its members may be willing, not only to encourage the school by regular attendance upon its

sessions and personal support of its program, but also to make such provision for its physical equipment and financial support as its needs may require.

(5) In order that his interest may be manifest to the pupils as well as to their teachers, he should as often as possible attend the sessions of the school or, if it is departmentally organized, visit the various departments. I heard recently of a little girl who, when requested by the superintendent of her department to attend the Sunday morning service of the Church, replied that, since her pastor was not interested in her services, she did not see why she should be interested in his. Of course Sunday school teachers should see to it that the members of their classes do not fall into the error of assuming that the Sunday school is a kind of children's Church and that the older people's Church is an altogether different thing, in which they need feel no vital concern. It will be much easier to do this, however, if the children are assured of the pastor's interest in them and in the work which they and their teachers are seeking to do.

(6) The pastor should see that the special evangelistic season recommended by the General Sunday School Board, or some other like period that he may find it expedient to select, is faithfully and diligently and intelligently observed. To this end he should call his officers and teachers together in advance for the study of plans and for such special organization as the work in hand may require. And especially should he see that the leaflet literature provided by the General Sunday School Board is not only put into the hands of

his officers and teachers, but also that they give to it such careful study as will enable them to incorporate its suggestions in their working program. During this entire special season the pastor should confer frequently with his officers and teachers in regard to all the details of the work, in order that he may have a perfect understanding of all that is done and may make sure that nothing that is essential is overlooked.

3. Attention has already been called to the fact that no group of persons, either old or young, should be received into the Church without definite instruction in regard to the meaning of the vows they are to assume and the nature and purpose of the institution with which they are to become associated. In this work of preparation the Sunday school teacher should be able to render valuable assistance. For reasons which are quite apparent, however, a large part of this responsibility should be undertaken by the pastor. In the first place, it will generally be found that he is the only person at hand who is thoroughly qualified for the task; but, even if this were not the case, it would still be unwise for a pastor to receive a group of persons, and especially a group of boys and girls, into the Church without first seeking through intimate personal association and conversation with them so to win their respect and confidence and affection as to enable them to realize in some measure the meaning of their relation to him as their spiritual leader and counselor.

The process of preparation should continue through at least a month, two hours being devoted to it each week. One of the much-needed additions to our educational literature is a graded series of guides to be used by pastors in training classes for Church membership. In the absence of such helps, it will devolve upon the pastor to prepare his own material. In order to do this, he should divide those who are to be received into three groups, classified according to age. The first group should comprise those under thirteen, the second those between fourteen and seventeen, and the third those over seventeen. The instruction given to each group will be determined both as to form and content by the capacities and needs of those composing it. In the case of children and youth it should be simple and concrete, both doctrines and practical precepts being illustrated and enforced by facts drawn from the history of the Church and the lives of distinguished religious leaders.

The vows of Church membership and the General Rules should be taken as the basis of instruction.* The former should be regarded as including the baptismal covenants, since they require the reaffirmation of these covenants. While it will be necessary in the instruction given to call attention to types of conduct that are inconsistent with the Christian ideal of living, the teaching should be predominantly positive. That is, it should interpret religion in terms of privilege and of opportunity for service rather than in terms of negation.

By way of giving some idea of what I have in mind,

---

*It is understood that in baptizing children and receiving them into the Church the pastor will use the ritual prepared specifically for this purpose and that upon this he will base his preparatory instruction.

let us assume that the pastor is undertaking the preparation of a group of junior boys and girls. His first step will, of course, be to get on the best possible terms with them. Too much care cannot be taken at this point. If the children are constrained and ill at ease in the pastor's presence, he will make but little progress in winning their interest and attention. He should seek, therefore, to make them feel that he is simply an older friend who really understands and cares for them and desires to help them to a richer and more useful and joyous life. Intimate personal conversation about things in which children are interested should have a large place in the entire training process. Through such heart-to-heart fellowship the pastor should seek to remove the embarrassment which boys and girls too often feel in talking with their elders about religion and to help them to understand that nothing is more natural and beautiful than that those who are just entering upon the great adventure of life should take Jesus as their Friend and Companion and should pledge to him their devoted and loyal service.

Having come to an understanding with the class, the pastor may well begin his course of instruction with a series of simple talks designed to deepen and vitalize the impressions made upon them in the previous educational process. In these conversations he should seek to draw from the children what they understand by faith and prayer and loyalty to Christ and to correct any misapprehensions into which they may have fallen. Of course this instruction should be as simple and concrete as it can possibly be made, since doctrines

208

that cannot be illustrated in terms of real life have but little meaning for boys and girls. By such a series of intimate conversations the pastor may make clear to the children what is involved in the first question which they will be required to answer when they are received into the Church and may thus enable them to answer sincerely and intelligently.

The series of talks about personal religion may be followed by a series of similarly adapted talks about the Church and its work. These should include a simple explanation of the big world-wide task to which the Church is committed and should interpret Church membership in terms of vital participation in this task. The series may well be concluded with a brief account of the origin and history of our own denomination, of the lives of a few of its conspicuous leaders, and of some of the important things it is now seeking to accomplish. By this instruction the class may be prepared intelligently to assume the second of the vows of Church membership.

It may be that in the course of these conversations the pastor will discover that some of the children, because of inadequate previous training, are not really ready to be received into the Church. In such cases, unless he finds it possible to awaken in them a deeper and more vital interest, it may be well for him to explain to them why he deems it necessary for them to continue in the class for a while longer. Of course children whose reception is thus delayed will need to be looked after carefully and sympathetically by both pastor and Sunday school teachers. For, while it is necessary

14   209

that children should clearly understand that joining the Church is a step which must be taken seriously and intelligently, it is also necessary to make sure that nothing is done that will tend to discourage those whose reception it may be found expedient to postpone.

Preparatory instruction for young people and adults will, of course, be adapted both as to content and method of presentation to their larger capacities and differing needs. It should include in a more fully elaborated form everything in regard to personal and practical religion that is included in the instruction of children; but it should also include such information in regard to matters of doctrine, polity, and history as are necessary for intelligent membership in the denomination into which the applicants are to be received. Perhaps it will be found best in most cases to deal with these older persons privately and individually rather than in groups.

Of course the success of the pastor in such an undertaking as is here suggested will depend upon his ability to draw vivid pictures, in terms that the child can comprehend, of characters, actions, and events that appeal to the normal interests of childhood. Any pastor, however, may acquire this ability, provided he is sufficiently impressed with the importance of the work to be willing thoroughly to familiarize himself with the material which he is to present and with the capacities and interests of those with whom he is to deal.

Courses for youth and for adults should cover the same general ground with such changes in viewpoint and teaching methods as the needs of the respective groups may require.

4. The training process should culminate on a given day set apart for receiving the applicants into the Church, and for this occasion the most careful preparation should be made. The whole order of service, including hymns, prayers, and Scripture readings, should be planned in advance and should be arranged with the view to enabling the children to take part in it. If the classes are sufficiently large, it is best to receive the juniors in one group, the intermediates and seniors in another, and the young people and adults in still another. After the several groups have been received, the holy communion should be administered, and a brief period should be given at the close of the service to an informal welcome to all on the part of the Church. Such a service following such a course of preparation may become a mountain top experience which the child or youth will recall with joy and gratitude throughout his entire life.

In a striking passage in one of his works Jean Paul Richter describes his first Lord's Supper, which in the Lutheran Church corresponds with our ceremony of receiving children into Church membership. He tells about the previous course of preparation and especially about the last meeting on the Saturday evening preceding the sacred service, when the warm tears which his beloved pastor shed mingled with those of the boys and girls as he prayed with them and for them.

"On this evening," he says, "there came a mild, light, clear heaven of peace over my soul, an unutterable

211

blessedness in feeling myself quite clean, purified, and freed from sin; in having made peace with God and man, a joyful far-reaching peace, and still, from these evening hours of mild and warm soul rest, I looked onward to the heavenly enthusiasm and rapture at the altar next morning.

"On Sunday morning the boys and girls, adorned for the sacrificial altar, met at the parsonage for the solemn entrance into the church amid singing and bell-ringing. . . . All this became for the young soul a powerful breeze in its outspread wings, which were already raised and in motion. Even during the long sermon the heart expanded with its fire, and inward struggles were carried on against all thoughts which were worldly or not sufficiently holy.

"At length I received the bread from my father and the cup from my purely loved teacher, but the ceremony did not receive any additional value from the thought of what these two were to me; my heart and mind and soul were devoted alone to heaven, to happiness, and to the reception of the Most Holy, which was to unite itself with my being, and my rapture rose to a physical lightning feeling of miraculous union.

"I thus left the altar with a clear blue infinite heaven in my heart; this heaven revealed itself to me by an unlimited, stainless, tender love which I now felt for all, all mankind. To this day I have preserved within my heart with loving and youthful freshness the remembrance of the happiness when I looked on the Church members with love, and took them all to my innermost heart.

"The whole earth remained for me throughout the day an unlimited love repast, and the whole tissue and web of life appeared to me an ethereal harp played by the breath of love."

Happy the man who amid the tumult and strife and temptations of later years can look back upon such an exalted experience as marking his formal entrance into the great brotherhood of believers! To be sure the emotional accompaniments of the occasion will necessarily vary with different individual types, but the ceremony of receiving any group of boys and girls into the Church may be so shot through with spiritual significance as to leave upon the soul even of the most prosaic child an impression which time can never erase.

5. I realize that the successful carrying out of such a program as I have here outlined will make large demands upon the time and strength of the pastor, already burdened by a distracting multiplicity of calls for all kinds of service. But I still raise the question as to whether or not his special work with the childhood and youth of his congregation is not one of the things which he cannot afford to omit, whatever else he may find it necessary to leave undone. For it is among these that he will find his chief opportunity for making real disciples and developing a nobler and more efficient type of Christian manhood and womanhood. Any one who will leave off theorizing and come face to face with the facts must see that under present conditions there is no hope for bringing about the triumph of the kingdom of God in any other direction.

213

The pastor, to be sure, should seek to become an effective preacher, but the pastor who believes that he can build up a really strong and vital Church through preaching alone and preaching that is directed mainly to adults is simply indulging in vain imaginings. For if the pastor is so intent upon feeding and tending the sheep that he neglects to feed and shepherd the lambs, there is danger that the time will come when he will find his flock sadly depleted in strength as well as in numbers.

V. IN CONCLUSION

In closing these studies I may be permitted once more to call attention to the fact that the responsibility of the Church does not cease when the child or youth or even the adult has been led to a definite surrender to Christ and welcomed into the Christian fellowship. The making of disciples is to be followed by teaching them to observe all things whatsoever Christ has commanded. And this involves a continuous and wisely adapted process both of instruction and training, to the end that those who have entered upon the Christian life may attain an ever-increasing intimacy with Christ, an ever-increasing likeness to Christ, an ever-increasing understanding of the principles proclaimed by Christ, and an ever-increasing ability to apply these principles in their social relations. In other words, it is the business of the Church to supply the conditions which will enable its new recruits, not only to come as individuals "unto the measure of the stature of the fullness of Christ," but also to attain the highest social efficiency.

This brings us back to the thought with which our studies began. Christianity regards the individual life as possessing infinite value and makes full provision for its emancipation and development. But it recognizes the fact that the individual can come to perfection only in a perfect social environment, and therefore charges the Church with the duty of saving, not the individual only, but society also. It is her business to bring about the realization of that divine event for which our Lord taught his disciples to pray: "Thy kingdom come. Thy will be done, as in heaven, so on earth." And this can be accomplished only by such a program of evangelism as I have sought to outline in these studies, a program which seeks to enlist the entire membership in the task of winning disciples, instructing them in the teachings of Christ, and training them in the application of these teachings to the concrete problems of individual and social life.

In this program the Church is to make use of all available agencies and methods and is to seek to reach people of all ages and conditions. Since, however, the method that lends itself to the widest application is the method of educational evangelism and the class that is most easily accessible is the childhood and youth of the world, it is plainly the part of wisdom for the Church to give to the evangelization of the young, through a wisely planned and intelligently directed process of religious education, that place of primacy in its work which its importance demands. Perhaps the fact that she has hitherto failed to do so may partly account for the threatened collapse of our civili-

215

zation which we witness to-day. It will furnish a measure of compensation, however, for all that we have suffered and are still suffering, if our bitter experiences shall serve to turn our attention to the latent possibilities of childhood and the means through which these possibilities may be brought to concrete realization. For in this direction lies hope for the Church and for the world. Out of the plastic material furnished us in the boys and girls who are playing and dreaming about us we may by the help of the Holy Spirit raise up a generation of men and women who will really represent Christ in the world and will usher in a civilization that will be dominated by the spirit of Christ, the spirit of brotherhood and service, and that will seek to regulate its social, business, and political life and its international relations by the principles of Christ. Thus and thus only may the bewildering problems that confront us to-day be solved.

SUGGESTIONS FOR STUDY

1. Why is the task of educational evangelism necessarily a coöperative task?

2. Make an outline of all the ways you can think of in which officers and teachers may coöperate.

3. Make a similar outline of ways of coöperation between the Sunday school and the home.

4. What relation has the Quarterly Conference to the evangelistic work of the Sunday school?

5. What place should the pastor have in it?

6. Do you agree that people should be carefully trained before being received into the Church? Give the reason for your answer.

7. How far do you agree with the statements contained in the last section of this chapter? Give your reasons.

216